KU-682-610

THE COUGAR BASIN WAR

Philip Ketchum

CHIVERS
THORNDIKE

This Large Print book is published by BBC Audiobooks Ltd, Bath, England and by Thorndike Press®, Waterville, Maine, USA.

Published in 2004 in the U.K. by arrangement with Golden West Literary Agency.

Published in 2004 in the U.S. by arrangement with Golden West Literary Agency.

U.K. Hardcover   ISBN 1–4056–3077–9 (Chivers Large Print)
U.K. Softcover   ISBN 1–4056–3078–7 (Camden Large Print)
U.S. Softcover   ISBN 0–7862–6828–X (Nightingale)

Copyright © 1970, by Philip Ketchum

All rights reserved.

The text of this Large Print edition is unabridged.
Other aspects of the book may vary from the original edition.

Set in 16 pt. New Times Roman.

Printed in Great Britain on acid-free paper.

British Library Cataloguing in Publication Data available

Library of Congress Control Number: 2004107030

KENT
ARTS & LIBRARIES

C 1525788 11

HE

DAR

16/11/17
HE

D
T   Ashen Drive Library
F   Tel/Fax: 01322 223556
d   − 1 DEC 2022

23. SEP 05   HLS
                (10) EJ   2 9 MAR 2010 − 3 JAN 2023
11/05   8 − JUL 2010   5/4/23
                                 3 1 JAN 2013   HE
2 8 AUG 2006   HARRIS
                                 2 8 NOV 2014
1 4 MAY 2007 WITHDRAWN 2015

Books should be returned or renewed by the
last date stamped above

KETCHUM   P

The Cougar Basin War

CHARTER MARK
Awarded for excellence

Yellow

Kent
County
Council

C152578811

I

It had been a good trip. When he had reached Mountain City he had run across two other horse wranglers and had joined th/em. They had hired five riders to help in the hunt and had set off in the high mesa country. Before ten days had passed they sighted the mustang band they were after. In two more weeks they trapped them, forty-four wild horses. Breaking them to a halter had not been easy.

Ben had picked out a dozen as his share. That was less than the others but he got his choice of the entire herd. He had selected twelve young mares. He was looking ahead, to the future, to the foals these young horses would produce. He had eight mares at home. A dozen more would keep his three stallions busy. Last year, in order to pay up some bills, he had sold most of his horses. The next two years would be building years.

This was his fourth and last day on the trail, headed home. He ought to make it over the final ridge by early afternoon. In another two hours he would be turning the mares into one of the corrals. He had been worried about the trip home. A dozen half wild horses could have been quite a problem. But the weather had been good and he had taken his time.

He made it to the last ridge shortly after

noon, and he stopped briefly when he got there. He always stopped at this point, going or coming. The view was worth it. Directly ahead, over the Ute Hills, was the vast, grass rich Cougar Basin. Beyond were scrubby hills, too far away to be seen. The land there and to the far left and far right was arid, and not of much value. The Cougar, however, was like an emerald jewel. None of it was his, but he could still enjoy it, ride through it. It was unspoiled cattle country.

He rode on, leading the string of mares behind him. He had not been able to see his own place in the Ute Hills, just ahead. There were too many low hills in the way, and there were too many trees. He had three small meadows near the ranch, and five corrals. The meadows were fenced and there were sheds over parts of three of the corrals. The other two would be partially covered eventually. The house, the cabin, the barn and the sheds were sufficient. Give him five more years of work and he ought to be financially sound. He had a good helper in Andy Thorne, who was there now, looking after things while he was away. A dependable man, Andy. He was not very imaginative and when he went to town he sometimes drank too much and got quarrelsome, but there were worse faults than that. Ben had been lucky to find him.

A painful memory had been gnawing at him most of the morning. Whenever he went away for a time, and came home, it seemed impossible not to remember Opal. He had never tried to forget her; he had never told himself that he had to put her out of his mind; he wouldn't want to. She had been a good wife—but she had died too soon, much too soon. When had he lost her? Two years ago. That seemed like a long time.

He scowled at the trail ahead. He was a tall young man, twenty-seven years old, but sometimes he felt older than that. He had wide shoulders, long powerful arms, and strong, well-shaped hands. He had quick reactions— he was fast with his gun, good with a rope. His face was thin, wind-tanned, with dark, well-spaced eyes, a humped nose, a tight-lipped mouth. There was a hint of stubbornness in the line of his jaw.

He shook off his memories now, straightened up and started looking forward to the moment when he would come through the trees to the end of the long, narrow meadow, and see across it the corrals and buildings of the ranch. Andy would be working outside, somewhere, or he might be in one of the downhill meadows. He would be glad when Ben arrived. Andy had never liked working alone.

The trees and shrubbery thinned out; the meadow was just ahead. Ben's eyes swept up toward the corrals and the ranch buildings and he reined in suddenly, gasped and shook his

3

head. A voice inside him cried out, *Oh, no! No! This is impossible! A fire—everything gone, even the horses!* But no, not the horses. If a fire had started and there had been a wind, every building might have been destroyed, but that should not have included the horses. The three corrals that he could see had been pulled down, and were empty, but the horses must have been moved somewhere else.

It wasn't warm, but he was sweating. He took a quick look up the meadow but there was nothing to see. He stared again at the gaunt, ugly ruins of the fire. What had been the house was nothing more than a pile of charred timbers and the ruins of a stone fireplace and chimney. He had said, boastfully, to Opal, that the chimney and fireplace would stand up forever. He had been terribly wrong about that. The barn, the cabin and sheds, even the two outhouses were in ruins. The fire had consumed everything, even the wood housing over the well.

The string of horses behind him were getting restive. He moved on, slanted across the meadow. He started shaking. It had taken a moment or two to realize the enormity of his loss. His horses might have been saved but everything else was gone—the buildings that had taken so long to build, the furnishings inside, clothing, furniture, blankets, rugs, even a piano.

Sudden tears came to his eyes and that

4

made him angry. He had taken a loss. This was like a hard blow to the stomach, at a time when he wasn't ready. It might stun him, but it would never knock him out unless he gave up, quit, stopped battling back. The thing to do now was to wipe out his tears, take a deep, steadying breath and look ahead, make a reassessment of what he faced and decide what to do next.

He tied the string of horses to one of the posts of the nearest corral, noticing at the time that most of the corral had been pulled down. It should not have been necessary to go that far to free the horses inside. To open the gate should have been enough, but then he hadn't been here at the fire, he hadn't seen how bad it was.

He tied his own horse with the others, then walked around what had been the yard. He tried to make a guess as to the date of the fire. It hadn't been the day before or the day before that. It might have been a week ago, or even two weeks ago. No longer than that. There were still traces of the men who had been here, attracted by the fire. He could see bootprints nearby, a good many bootprints. If the fire had been more than two weeks ago, the traces of the men who had been here would have almost vanished.

But there was work to be done. He had come back with a dozen mustang mares and needed a place to hold them. The rest of the

5

afternoon was used up in rebuilding one of the corrals, and getting water from the well. Then he spent a little time, prowling the ruins of the house. And he did some thinking about what had caused the fire. It might have been the result of lightning, or Andy accidentally knocking over a lighted lamp. There was another possibility—that the fire had been started deliberately. He didn't want to think of such a thing, but why had three of his corrals been so completely destroyed? Someone had torn down long sections of the fences. Why? How could he account for a thing like that?

There was still light in the sky; it would be another hour until dark. He had time to check the other corrals, a mile or two away. He mounted his horse, headed down through the hills. In a quarter of an hour he reached the first downhill corral. It was empty; a good half of the fence had been pulled down. He rode on to the last corral. It had been destroyed just like the others. If only the corrals had been empty, he might have thought his horses had been moved or stolen; but the pulling down of the fences seemed to indicate something else. Who hated him this much?

He thought of two men almost at once, Jeff Lorimer and Henry Matthews, but after a moment's consideration he shook his head. Although it seemed as though his corrals had been deliberately destroyed, he didn't know, factually, what had happened. What he ought

6

to do, first, was find and talk to Andy Thorne—if he was still around. Or if he wasn't, then he ought to talk to the sheriff, or to some of the men who had come here after the fire.

He wheeled around, headed back to the ranch. It was a long trip down through the hills, then across the basin to Benjamin. He would head for town in the morning—to make the trip now would be senseless. Fred Gibbons, the sheriff, was an aging man, would have turned in early. He might find a few people to talk to in the saloon, but he couldn't be sure who'd be there.

He came back to the place where he had once lived, dismounted, unsaddled his horse. He had a few supplies left in his saddlebags, enough for a scanty meal. He was standing over his cookfire when he heard the sound of horses headed his way, and he looked up and saw three men riding toward him.

They were still some distance away, headed up the meadow. At first he guessed they were from the basin but as they drew closer, it hit him abruptly that they were strangers.

His rifle was in its boot, leaning across his blanket roll, several steps away. He was wearing his handgun; it was in his holster. He touched it casually, just to be sure it was there.

The three men pulled up quite close to the fire and one spoke, a thin, hunched, tired-looking man. His voice had a high twang. 'Just in time for supper, huh?'

'It'll be a poor meal,' Ben answered. 'I've been away; don't have much grub left.'

The man leaned forward. 'Is your name Ben Carnaby?'

'Yes, that's my name. How did you . . .'

He broke off what he was saying, aware that three guns were covering him. He had noticed the motions of the men's arms and he could have grabbed for his own gun, but in the face of odds like this it would have been foolish. Besides, he had no idea what this was all about. He stood tense, waiting.

The man who had been doing the talking, spoke again. 'That's right, Carnaby. Hold steady while Taft drops down and gets your gun. Try anything, and you get blasted.'

Ben moistened his lips. 'What do you want with me?'

'Not much,' the man said. 'Just do what I tell you. Right now, just keep steady.'

One of the other men had dismounted. He gave the reins of his horse to the third man, holstered his gun and started circling to get behind Ben. This man, Taft, was heavy, wide-shouldered; he might have been in his late thirties. He had puffy cheeks, small dark eyes and enough whiskers to make his face look dirty. It might have been dirty anyhow. The man passed the fire and out of range of Ben's eyes.

Ben had started sweating. He heard Taft's footsteps moving up behind him and it wasn't easy, just to stand there. If he waited, motionlessly, he might lose only his gun—but he might get something else, a knife in the back, a heavy blow over the head.

The thin, hunched man motioned with his gun. 'That's it, Carnaby. Just hold steady and everything'll be fine.'

Ben was tense, scarcely breathing. Taft moved up behind him, even closer. He grabbed for the holstered gun. Ben was well aware of that but he sensed something else, the swinging of Taft's arm into the air. The man slammed it down and Ben jerked his head, tried to avoid the blow that was coming. He almost managed it. The gun Taft was holding crashed against the side of Ben's head, just above the temple.

Pain swept over him. He pitched forward, but a heavy, thick darkness seemed to swallow everything.

*   *   *

'Now, take it easy,' Andy said. 'Lay down where you was. Ain't nothing you can do now.'

'Where am I?' Ben asked.

'In a camp I set up eight or nine days ago. It's in the trees east of where the ranch house used to be.'

Ben eased down. His head hurt terribly. Until a few minutes ago he had been unconscious. He had no notion what time it

9

was, but it was dark.

'Where did you find me?' Ben asked.

'You was near the ruins of the house,' Andy answered. 'Got back late from town, rode up through the meadow, cut by near the house. Heard you groaning or I would have missed you. What happened to your head?'

'A man named Taft is responsible for that.'

'Taft?' Andy said. 'Taft? Never heard of him.'

'Didn't you notice the horses?' Ben asked. 'I brought back a dozen mustang mares. I put them in the north corral. Part of the fence had been torn down but I set it up again.'

Andy was silent, a dark, lumpy figure seated nearby.

'You mean you didn't notice the horses?' Ben asked.

'Nope. I didn't,' Andy said gruffly.

Ben scowled. He fingered his bandaged head and thought: *The mares are gone. Taft and the other men took them. I should have expected it.*

He looked at Andy. 'What started the fire?'

'I don't know.' The man took a deep breath and he seemed to be bracing himself. 'I wasn't here. I had gone into town. I didn't do that more'n five times while you were gone, but that was when we had the fire. Gibbons said I was lucky I wasn't here the day of the fire. It was outlaws that set the place afire. They took the horses, too.'

'Outlaws!' Ben tried to say it quietly. 'What outlaws?'

'Don't know. Maybe the same men you ran into today. You ain't said anything about them but you didn't bang up your own head and you said you brought back some mares. I sure didn't see them.'

'Did the sheriff try to get back my horses?'

'Sure did. I rode with him and about six other men.' Andy shook his head. 'We didn't even get in sight of them. Followed them into the *malpais* hills, maybe fifty miles.'

'Off to the west?'

'North and west. That's sure rotten country. After we got back I moved out here and camped, waited for you. Wasn't much sense in doing that but I did.'

Ben was quiet for a time. His head hurt terribly. It was hard to think clearly. Several half-formed questions had started to shape up in his mind. He seized on one—the outlaws. This was something new to the basin. As far as he knew the people around here had never been troubled by rustlers, highwaymen, or those who lived outside the law. What outlaw band had found its way to the basin? Where had they gone? Would they ever be back? What about the three men who had jumped him tonight? Were they the ones who had burned out his place, stolen his horses? Maybe they were, but why had they been interested in his name?

He closed his eyes, leaned back.

'That's right,' Andy said. 'Try to get a little sleep.'

'I want to head for town tomorrow,' Ben said.

Andy nodded. 'Figured you would.'

'What's happened during the past two months?'

'Nothing much.' Andy motioned with his hands. 'How would I know if there had been any changes? Hardly ever get to town, and that's a fact. Ask anyone.'

He sounded defensive, and maybe with reason. He had said he had been in town five times since Ben had been away. Double that, and he might have been near the truth, but in spite of that Ben knew he had no legitimate reason to criticize him for the fire or the loss of the horses. As the sheriff had said, if Andy had been here when the outlaws rode in, he probably would have been killed.

Ben touched his bandaged head. 'Thanks for looking after me.'

'I go away at the wrong times,' Andy said. 'The day of the fire, and again tonight.'

'You found me.'

'Did that by accident,' Andy said. Then he hesitated, but asked finally, 'Know what you're gonna do about the ranch? Gonna rebuild?'

'I'd like to.' He said that almost without thinking.

'Maybe you won't be needing me.'

12

'I'll be needing you. At least I'll be needing you if I can work things out.'

Until right now he had not thought about any of the practical problems now facing him. He still owed just over a thousand dollars to the bank in Benjamin. If he wanted to rebuild the ranch, get started again, he was going to need three thousand dollars more. George Matthews might turn him down, or he might not. The man had never liked Ben, but above his personal feelings Matthews was a good businessman. That had always been his first consideration. It was worthwhile talking to him.

'If we're heading in to town tomorrow, we better get some rest,' Andy said.

'Sure. We'll talk in the morning,' Ben answered.

He closed his eyes, tried to relax. His head still hurt pretty badly, but he ought to feel better by morning. He would wait for the light—and for the chance to trail the three men who had stolen the mares. He had told Andy he was going to town, and he meant it, but there was no hurry about getting there. Another chore came first.

II

Ben woke up as it was growing light. The pounding head pain that had bothered him the night before was gone. In its place was a sick, whipped feeling. The source of it was his realization of what he had lost while he had been away—the burning of his ranch buildings, the destruction of his corrals, the disappearance of his livestock. He could build again, buy the things he needed, buy more horses, go on another mustang hunt, but things like that took time and money. He had the time to start again. The question now was whether he could get the money from George Matthews. Matthews had never really liked him, had never forgiven him for marrying Opal.

Ben got up, glanced toward Andy's lumpy figure. He was still asleep. Ben didn't bother him. Wood had already been gathered. He started a fire in the fire ring, found the coffeepot, noticed where the creek was and walked there to get water for coffee. Andy's camp was located not far from the burned-down ranch buildings, but back in the trees and out of sight.

Andy was up by the time Ben returned. He had started breakfast, and he looked up and said, 'Thanks for the fire. Want to start it

14

every morning?'

'Nope. That's your job,' Ben answered. 'Did those men take my horse?'

'Could be. Didn't look around last night but didn't notice your horse anywhere.'

'Do you have an extra?'

'Nope. We might have to ride double. You can probably rent a horse from Ackerman, in town.'

'It's closer to Rowland's.'

'Oh, I forgot to tell you.' Andy added more wood to the fire, set a frying pan in place and put some thick bacon into it. He looked up again. 'Rowland's gone. He sold his place to a couple of Texans. I think one is named Bryan; the other is Chico Kelly.'

'So Rowland's gone. His wife too?'

'Yep—maybe to the sorrow of Jeff Lorimer.'

Andy was reaching into a bag of gossip in making a statement like that. Ben's ranch was in the lower Ute Hills. Just beyond the hills and on the fringe of the Cougar Basin was Rowland's. He had not had a large ranch but he seemed satisfied with it. Beyond his range was Lorimer's much larger place. From what people said, Jeff was overly interested in Andy's wife. Now, of course, that made little difference. The Rowlands were gone.

'So we have new neighbors,' Ben said slowly. 'Two Texans, a man named Bryan and another called Chico Kelly. What are they like?'

15

'Hardly know them,' Andy replied.

'I thought you said nothing much had happened while I was away.'

'Didn't think about the Rowlands moving out.'

Ben had handed the coffeepot to Andy. It was now sitting in the fire, being heated. He couldn't smell the coffee yet but he could smell the bacon and it reminded him that it was good to be alive and able to think about food. He backed away from the fire, sat down and waited for breakfast, and wondered about Jeff Lorimer and Ellen. Jeff was about fifty, a widower. There had been a time when people had thought that Jeff Lorimer and Iron Kate Salter, whose ranch was east of the river, would get together. They were about the same age—a woman without a husband and a man without a wife. Iron Kate's ranch was almost as large as Jeff's. It could have been a fifty-fifty deal, excepting for the fact that Iron Kate and Jeff hated each other. Jeff had told Ben once that someday he might get married again, but he never had. And it could be that he was interested in Ellen Rowland. She had been a rather nice person, much nicer than her husband.

He shook his head. That was in the past, something to forget. The Rowlands were gone and as a result he had new neighbors, two Texans. That is, he had two new neighbors if he could manage to hang onto his ranch.

*　　*　　*

They had breakfast, straightened up the camp, then Andy saddled up, mounted his horse and took the time to look around the ruins of the ranch house and into the nearby trees to see if he could find Ben's horse. He didn't. The horse was gone.

'They took him, of course,' Ben said. 'And my mares. Which way did they head? Off to the *malpais*, to the badlands to the west?'

'Nope. Don't think so,' Andy said. 'At least, from the way I can read it they headed toward the basin. Could be they'll turn west afore long.'

Ben nodded. That seemed to be a good guess. The outlaws, leading a stolen horse and a string of wild mustang mares, surely wouldn't head to where they would be seen. Another thought occurred to him. It might be that the outlaws wouldn't be leading the mares very far. The average man wouldn't know how to handle mustangs.

'We'll get started,' Ben said abruptly. 'Let's see where the men went.'

'If they head for the badlands and we go after them, we'll need more grub and water,' Andy said. 'And we ought to get us another horse.'

'But first we'll see where they headed,' Ben decided.

17

He climbed up behind Andy and they started off, picking up the trail of the outlaws south of Ben's home meadow. It was easy to follow them. The outlaws had left a wide trail. The mustang mares, still unused to a halter and not accustomed to following in line, must have given the outlaws trouble almost from the first. From the signs he could read the mares had swung from side to side, then they must have charged ahead, fighting to get free. In less than three miles the outlaws must have given up, set the mares free. They had scattered in every direction. By this time they were long gone, headed back into the hills. It would have taken an army, and at least a month to catch even some of them.

'So what do we do now?' Andy asked.

'Follow the trail of the men,' Ben answered. 'They're still headed for the basin.'

'I still think they'll cut off toward the badlands,' Andy said.

He was wrong. The trail of the three men leading one extra horse continued down through the hills and into the open stretches of the basin. This had been Harry Rowland's range, now the property of two Texans. Ben noticed a good many cattle. Those he came close to were still wearing Rowland's cattle brand, the *Double R*. The Texans might have bought the brand; certainly they must have bought the cattle.

In another mile or two they would cut

across a corner of Rowland's land and reach the road that stretched up the basin; the trail of the outlaws still pointed in that direction. Ben mentioned it, then said, 'What do you think now, Andy? Could they be headed for town?'

'I guess they could,' Andy admitted. 'But they're damn fools for risking it.'

'Why? They might look like three ordinary strangers. Hope we run into them.'

'We probably won't. Couldn't be that lucky. You sure you'll know them?'

'I'll know them.'

'Didn't you work for the sheriff once?'

'About three years ago, when he broke his leg. I took his place for about four months.'

'Think he might be able to help you?'

'I think he'd like to, if it didn't push him into a corner, if the job wasn't too hard.' Ben was silent for a moment, thinking about Sheriff Fred Gibbons, who was lately carrying his years heavily. Ben spoke again. 'He was one of the early pioneers, quite a firebrand when he was younger.'

'Plan to see him?'

'Soon as I can. I want to see Matthews, too.'

'I never liked him.'

'Not many people do. He's as cold as the dead of winter, but if you go to him with a good solid proposition to make money, he'll loan you what you need.'

'For ten percent interest.'

'That's his cut, Andy. Not as high as the average outlaw.'

'I still don't have to like him,' Andy said.

They rode on, now and then talking, but most of the time they were silent. They passed Rowland's land, came to the road and followed it. Several times they saw other riders, but at a distance. To their left now was the Cougar River. Its headwaters were to the north, behind them, in the Madre Mountains. The stream curved past Red Mesa, skirting the Ute Hills. After the river passed through the basin it continued on to the Gila and at that point was forgotten. On down the basin, and just past the place where Chaparral Creek joined the Cougar, they would come to the town of Benjamin. They ought to get there early in the afternoon.

Right now, and until they reached the town, they would be riding between Jeff Lorimer's range and the range belonging to Iron Kate Salter. Actually, the river was the border between these two big ranches in the basin. There were other ranches in the fringes of the basin, and three more on Red Mesa, but the best land was along the river.

When Ben came here six years ago, he had gone to work first for Jeff Lorimer, and he had worked there for two years. That last year he had fallen in love with Opal Lorimer. Then, quite abruptly, and for no reason Lorimer would ever understand, he had left Lorimer and gone to work for Iron Kate. To Lorimer it must have seemed that he had joined the enemy. Actually, he hadn't. He had gone to work for Iron Kate because she made such a good proposition he couldn't turn it down. She promised to provide the cattle and the land to start a ranch for himself, off toward Red Mesa. But things had not worked out that way. Iron Kate had stalled about his land, and the cattle he was to get as part of his wages. Eventually it seemed he would never get anything from Iron Kate. There were too many strings on every offer. After a year and a half he quit her.

That was when he headed to town and took Gibbon's place as sheriff. He spent four months at that—four interesting months. During that time he had made a few friends—but more enemies. It was during that time that he came up with the idea of starting a horse ranch in the Ute Hills. He had saved the money to buy the land, and George Matthews put up the money for the horses. Ben had wanted a chance for himself—and he did all right. He had married Opal but then she had suddenly died. At that point he had almost quit, but in some way or other he had been able to pull himself together, and go on. Here was his second tragedy, his second defeat, looking at him right now—the loss of his ranch buildings and livestock. He had been slapped down hard. He could now appreciate how Andy felt about himself. He had said once, bitterly, *'Just look at me, Ben. I'm thirty-two, but what have I got to show for it? No ranch, no cattle, no money in the bank. I've had three good chances to get ahead but none of them worked out. I might never get another chance.'*

Ben thought about Andy. He was average sized but he stooped slightly. His hair was getting a little thin. He had powerful arms, big hands, and could do anything around the ranch—but often he had to be prompted. And he drank too much. He admitted that openly. Maybe his trouble was that he had accepted defeat, that he was through fighting.

Andy had reached for his gun, was checking it, when Ben asked, 'What you worried about?'

'Those three outlaws.' He stared ahead. 'We're almost to town. First thing we get there you better buy a gun.'

'It's on my list,' Ben answered.

'Want to carry my rifle?'

'I don't feel that desperate. Not yet.'

'You need a horse, too.'

'I'll talk to Ackerman at the livery stable. That's a good place to stop.'

Andy nodded. Ben could not see his face but he was sure the man was scowling.

They reached the edge of town, rode on in toward the plaza. The main street in Benjamin was the Plaza Square, four streets around a small park. This was the busy center of town. Back of the plaza were other streets and the houses of the town. Anything of importance

22

fronted on the plaza—including the livery stable, and even Laura's which had no other name and probably needed no other name.

Ben and Andy, riding double, passed several people who looked at them curiously. They came to the plaza, turned in the direction of the livery stable. Here and there along the hitching rails were a number of saddle horses. Ben saw several men he knew, but they were at a distance. He waved to one—Dave Eckert, who worked for Iron Kate.

'Here we are,' Andy said, and he turned into the saddling area in front of the livery stable.

Ben slid to the ground, stretched, flexed his muscles. He wasn't used to riding without the support of a saddle. He was almost stiff.

Andy dismounted, and led his horse toward the water trough.

Rod Ackerman stepped out from the barn. He glanced toward Andy, then looked at Ben and called out, 'Howdy there, Ben. Any luck on the high mesas?'

'Some fine mares,' Ben answered. 'But I lost them.'

'Tough. And I'm sorry about that fire. They tell me it was outlaws.'

'That's what I heard.'

'Where's your horse?'

'Lost him. Have you got one I can use?'

'Sure have. Need a saddle?'

'Everything.'

'I'll have one ready whenever you want him.'

23

'Many thanks.'

'Stall him near Andy's, near the door. We might want to ride out tonight.'

Ackerman nodded. He was short and because of the way he stooped he seemed even shorter. He was in his sixties. He had a white fringe around his head and a thin, stringy beard. Ben had got to know him rather well while he had served as sheriff. He had spent many a night here, just talking. He liked the way the man thought—more honestly than most men. And he could be brutally frank. Like Gibbons, he was another of the early pioneers. He had known this territory when the Indians had been the enemy.

'I'll take care of Andy's horse,' Ackerman said. 'Drop by and see me.'

'I will if I can,' Ben answered. 'Is Gibbons in town?'

'You ought to find him at his house. He's got a deputy running the office.'

'Is Jeff Lorimer here?'

'Yep. Somewhere.'

'Iron Kate?'

'Nope.'

'One more question. Did three strangers ride in early this morning? They might have brought an extra horse with them.'

'Several new men have moved into the basin,' Ackerman said. 'Some ride for the Texans. Don't know about the others. I'd like to help you, Ben, but I don't know the men you mean.'

Ben shrugged. 'Thanks, anyhow. I might drop by later.'

He turned away, headed for the plaza and crossed it. He was on his way to the hardware store for a new gun. With Andy beside him, Ben bought the handgun he wanted, a .45 Colt. It had a good balance, seemed to feel right in his hand. He slid it into the holster, making sure it didn't fit too tightly.

'Want to see the sheriff, next?' Andy asked, as they stepped outside.

Ben nodded. 'I thought I might.'

'Then you won't need me,' Andy said. 'I want you to talk to the sheriff alone. He might want to say something about me. While you're with him I'll nose around and see what I can find out.'

'Good idea,' Ben said. But he knew what Andy meant to do first—head for the saloon.

'I'll pick you up after you leave the sheriff's,' Andy promised.

'Or I'll find you.'

'Be a little careful, Ben.'

'Sure, I'll be careful.'

Andy turned away, hitched up his trousers, touched his holstered gun lightly, then headed up the street. One of the town's two saloons was at the corner. He reached it in record time.

Ben watched Andy walk out of sight, then he recrossed the plaza, noticing Jeff Lorimer

25

and one of his men standing in front of the hotel porch. He would have to pass them as he left the plaza, and that meant he would have to say something. It was never easy, anymore, to get along with Lorimer. The man never understood why Ben had quit his job, then went to work with Iron Kate. Later, when Ben had married Lorimer's only child, he had been furious. Lorimer never forgave him, or her. When she died suddenly he had cried out that Ben had been responsible. And he was still bitter, unforgiving. Ben tried to avoid him when he could. When they did meet the experience was never pleasant.

He braced himself, moved on toward Lorimer. The man with Jeff was Rusty Davis, a tall, thin man in his mid-thirties who never had much to say. Jeff was in his fifties, tall, heavy, well-muscled. He had dark hair and a thick, black beard. He was not an aggressive man, but he had a quick temper that sometimes resulted in trouble.

He stiffened as Ben approached, his eyes as stony as ever. He made a grating comment. 'Thought you'd left the basin.'

'Not yet,' Ben answered. Then he said, 'I was burned out. Maybe you heard about it. I understand some outlaws were responsible. Have they bothered you?'

'No.' Jeff was definite. 'I stay on the job, don't neglect things that're important.'

This was a veiled reference to his daughter's

26

death. She had died of pneumonia, in the winter. Jeff had said she would never have been sick if she stayed inside when it was bitterly cold. But Ben knew she wanted to work outside, helping him.

Jeff looked away. He asked flatly, 'What you gonna do now? Try to borrow money so you can get another start?'

'Might have to do that,' Ben admitted.

'You won't make it. One raid, and you got wiped out. Who's gonna take a chance on you again?'

'You could, Jeff.'

'Nope. Not me. Never. And you won't get any help from Matthews; you can bet on that.'

'It's still worth talking to him.'

'Nope. It's a waste of time. But talk to him if you want to. Try to hang on. I'll be watching what happens.'

'You do that,' Ben said, and he nodded to Rusty Davis, then moved on past the two men to the corner.

Fred Gibbons lived just a street away from the plaza. It took only a few minutes to reach it. Ben climbed to the porch, knocked on the door and waited. He knocked again and waited. It was moving on toward mid-afternoon, the time when Gibbons liked to rest. It wasn't the best time to see him, but Ben couldn't wait until evening.

He knocked on the door again, and a few moments later heard a grumbling voice inside.

27

Finally the door opened and the sheriff looked out at him. He was in his trousers and stockinged feet, his suspenders over the top of his underwear. He wasn't wearing a shirt. His thin, dark hair was rumpled from the pillow. He was big, almost fat. He never moved very fast. When he was younger he must have been considerably different.

'Oh, it's you,' Gibbons said. 'You ought to remember I always take a rest in the afternoon.'

'Sorry, Fred,' Ben said, and he smiled. 'How've you been?'

'Don't have the energy I used to have. What's so damned important?'

'What happened to my ranch?'

Gibbons wiped his hand over his face. He jerked his head. 'Come on in. Take a chair. Want a drink?'

Ben followed the man into the house. He took a chair, sat down, but he shook his head about a drink. 'Andy and I missed dinner; I think I'll skip the drink.'

'Andy wouldn't have skipped it, but he rode with me when we went after the men who burned you out.'

'Who were they?'

'Don't know. They headed into the badlands. We followed them for more'n fifty miles. Never got near them.'

'How many were there?'

'Four.'

28

'What did they do with my horses?'

'Turned them loose soon as they found out we was chasing them. I guess most of the horses must have headed for the hills. They might have made it. It was a crazy thing to chase them into the *malpais*. They never could have made it across.'

'Not without extra water,' Ben said.

'Mind if I get a drink?'

'Go ahead.'

The sheriff left the room, headed for the kitchen. Ben waited, scowling. He was taking a careful look at what had happened to him. Four men had raided his ranch. They could have taken the horses without burning down the buildings and tearing down the corrals. It was questionable that the outlaws had been after his horses at all. They had started into the badlands. It was an almost impossible trip across that kind of country without extra water. Most likely, after a day's drive, the horses had been set free. This was like last night. Three outlaws had jumped him, knocked him out, and had left with a string of wild mares. In a short distance they had been set free. Maybe it had been outlaws who had burned him out, but it looked as though the man responsible for it had some other motive for the raid. A man who hated him or who wanted to hurt him.

Gibbons came back with his drink. He settled down, and asked, 'Sure you don't

29

want one?'

'Not today,' Ben answered. 'Did you ever hear of an outlaw named Taft?'

'Taft? Taft?' The man blinked at his drink. 'Seems like I saw a poster with that name on it—I think it came from somewhere in Texas.'

'Where is the poster?'

'In my office, most likely. I'll look it up when I go down there, toward sundown.'

'Haven't you got a new deputy? Andy said so.'

'Yep. Name's Fowler.'

'You don't mean Brazos Fowler?'

'Could be that's his name.' Gibbons took a drink, gulped it, then said, muttering it, 'A man's got to take what he can get. Looked for a couple a weeks for a deputy, couldn't get one, then this man came along.'

Ben was silent. He stared out at nothing, trying to fit this bit of news into the picture. Brazos had been here before. He was a gunfighter who lived on the edge of the law. He had built up most of his reputation in Texas, where, it was said, he was wanted by the Rangers. He was a man in his forties, tall, thin, gaunt—and deadly. He could demand a high price if there was a cattle war going on; it was hard to understand why he would accept a deputy's salary, which was not much better than cowhand wages.

'He's not so bad,' Gibbons said defensively. 'I don't want you to cross him, Ben.'

'Don't worry.' Ben shook his head. 'I'm not looking for his kind of trouble. When you get to the office, look up Taft. I want to see the poster.'

'I'll dig it up,' Gibbon said.

Ben got to his feet. He was still trying to see some kind of pattern in what had happened to him, and he said, 'Texas. Brazos is from Texas and you tell me that Taft might have come from there. Then, there are two men who just moved into the basin and took Rowland's place. They're from Texas.'

'Lots of folks come from Texas,' Gibbons said. 'Have you met Eddie Bryan or Chico Kelly?'

'Not yet.'

'You'll like them. Fine, upstanding men.'

'Hope I do.'

'Sure sorry about what happened to your ranch,' Gibbons said. 'But there wasn't nothing we could do. By the time anyone got there the buildings were gone—the outlaws, too.'

'That's what Andy said.'

'You gonna manage to get started again?'

'I'll try to.'

'Good for you. Any way I can help you, just let me know.'

'Thanks,' Ben said.

He headed for the door, stepped outside, and for a moment stood there, reviewing what he had learned from Fred Gibbons. It amounted to very little—the fact that there

31

was a record on Taft. He had learned one other thing—Brazos Fowler had been hired as deputy—and there was something to worry about. The man was a killer. And now, wearing a badge, he could justify using his gun. He was a man to be avoided—if that was possible.

III

Ben walked back to the plaza and almost the moment he got there he saw Dave Eckert, to whom he'd waved earlier, and Tish Wellington, standing in the park. Tish was from Red Mesa, where she lived with her parents. She was a vivid twenty and very much alive. She had warm brown eyes and brown hair. In Ben's opinion she could not have been improved. He knew he could have fallen in love with her very easily. If he saw her more often he would. That thought ran through his mind, but right afterward he decided this wasn't the time to fall in love.

'Hey there, Ben,' Dave called. 'Been looking for you.'

'Here I am,' Ben said as he joined them. He turned to the girl. 'What brought you to town?'

'A horse that could outrun any horse you ever had.' Her eyes were bright, laughing.

'You must be referring to Big Red,' Ben said.

She nodded. 'You ought to try him some day.'

'I'd like to.'

Her expression changed quickly as she said, 'Ben, I'm terribly sorry about the fire. It was cruel to boast about my horse. Will you forgive me?'

'I already have,' Ben said.

'What are you going to do?'

'Start again.'

Dave Eckert broke in. 'Why not listen to me for a change? I've got a message for you.'

'A message?' Ben said. 'Go ahead.'

'Kate wants to see you.'

'That so?'

'Yep. Right away,' Dave said. 'I don't mean you've got to rush out to the ranch right now. But don't put it off too long.'

Ben was frowning. 'Know what she wants?'

'Nope. She didn't say.' Dave seemed to hesitate, then he added, 'Give her a chance, Ben. I know you had a row with her a couple of years ago but she's changed a lot. She's not as hard as she used to be.'

Ben wasn't sure of that. He wasn't even sure it was wise to go out and see her. She had told him, just before he left, never to even cross her land. She never wanted to see him. At least she must have changed her mind about that.

'I'll try to see her in a day or so,' Ben said slowly.

'Fine. I'll tell her,' Dave said, and he turned toward Tish. 'Nice to see you again. Drop by at the ranch, anytime. You're one of Kate's favorite persons.'

'I'll be by,' Tish said.

Dave turned away, headed across the plaza. That left Ben and Tish momentarily alone.

34

The girl looked at him curiously. 'What did you and Kate fight about, or isn't it any of my business?'

'It isn't,' Ben said, grinning, 'but I don't mind telling you. I worked for Kate for almost a year and a half. I was to get wages, plus four cows a month to be branded as mine. In two years I was to be given enough range to start a small ranch—my own. If I continued to work for Kate I would continue to get half wages for half time work, plus two cows a month.'

The girl was frowning. 'That was a strange agreement.'

'Yes, it was, but Kate was desperate for help. Everyone but Dave had quit her. It was a hot, dry year; some of the cattle were sick. I never worked harder in my life.'

'What did you fight about?'

'Kate didn't keep our bargain.'

'What would she say if I asked her what happened?'

'Ask her and find out. That might be interesting.'

Tish was still frowning. 'You said you were going to rebuild the ranch. Is it going to be easy?'

'No. It won't be.'

'It still isn't my business, but I suppose you need money.'

'Yes, I'll need money.'

'Kate might help.'

He shook his head slowly. 'No, I don't think

35

she'll do that. I have no idea why she wants to see me.'

Tish was silent for a moment and as they stood there Ben noticed two women starting across the park. They would pass near where he and Tish were standing. One of the women was Laura Digby, the other, he thought, was one of her girls. He had never seen her before. She was quite young and rather pretty.

Tish had noticed the two women. She turned away, looked in the other direction. She had stiffened, her face set in disapproving lines. Her lips were a tight, thin line.

The women moved nearer. Laura admitted she was thirty-five. She might have been older, but she kept herself in good condition. She looked like quite a woman. Ben had got to know her when he had been acting as sheriff. She had helped him several times. He rather liked her, and now he touched his hat. 'Hello, Laura.'

She smiled, nodded, stopped for a moment and said, 'Hello, Ben. I'm glad you're back. Sorry about what happened to your ranch.' She motioned to the girl with her. 'This is Jennie.'

She didn't speak but Ben said, 'Hello, Jennie. Hope you like it here.' Then some perverse impulse made him say, 'Tish, this is Laura Digby and one of her girls, Jennie.'

Tish turned toward them. She looked a little sick and she made some murmuring sound.

36

Laura frowned and nodded. Jennie said nothing. And right away Laura and Jennie moved on. In another moment they were across the plaza.

Tish spoke under her breath. 'I could slap you for that, Ben Carnaby.'

'Why?' Ben asked. 'What did I do wrong? Like them or not, they're people.'

'How well do you know Laura Digby?' She sounded furious.

'Quite well.'

'I'm surprised you admit it.'

'Why not? It's the truth. I met her when I was acting sheriff. A man who had broken into one of the stores hid there—in Laura's place. I went after him but Laura stopped me. She admitted the man was there with one of the girls. She was afraid that if I went in after him the girl might be hurt, and she could have been hurt. Laura wanted me to wait outside until the man left. That's what I did.'

'I suppose you met her other times.'

'Want to hear about it?'

'No.'

She was still furious. Ben was half sorry about what he had done. Maybe he should have overlooked the presence of Tish Wellington—but why? There were people like Laura in nearly every town; they were a fact of life. It was time to be honest about them.

Laura and Jennie had disappeared in a store but someone else caught his attention—a man standing near the barber shop. He was tall, thin, and his hat was tipped forward, shading most of his face. At the moment he was lounging easily against the building. It was Brazos Fowler. If Ben stayed around town it was inevitable that he'd meet him. That shouldn't bother him at all, but it did.

Tish spoke suddenly. 'I have to find Father. It's time to start home.' She looked straight at him. 'Ben, sometimes you make me angry. I don't know why you can't be different.'

He tried not to smile. 'How different?'

'I don't know. I suppose if you didn't do what you do, then you wouldn't be you.'

'Now, what does that mean?'

'You figure it out, Ben. I've got to find Father.' She whirled away, started across the plaza.

Ben headed for the bank, where he found George Matthews at a desk just back of the counter. That was where he spent most of the day. When an important person came to the bank Matthews usually took him into his private office. The average person never saw it. Ben was average. He had never been in Matthew's office. Even when he had arranged a three thousand dollar loan, to start the horse ranch, the deal had been handled over the counter.

He was really surprised, then, as Matthews stood up, pointed toward his office. 'We'll go in there, Carnaby. It's more private.'

He opened the gate so Ben could move back of the counter, then led the way to his office. He was short but wide-shouldered, and he stood very straight as though to claim every inch of height he could. He was in his late forties, a man with a brusque, incisive manner. His office was plainly furnished: a desk, a table, several chairs, a file case and bookcase. There was a worn carpet on the floor. The papers on his desk were neatly piled.

He took a seat at his desk, pointed to a nearby chair. 'Sit down, Carnaby. Sorry about your fire. I suppose this means you won't be able to pay what you owe the bank.'

'Not necessarily,' Ben answered. 'Your bank loaned me three thousand dollars. Counting the interest I've paid, I've returned well over two thousand.'

'What about what you still owe us?'

'It'll be paid.'

'How?'

'You're driving at me too fast,' Ben said. 'Why don't we slow down? As you said, I've had a fire. I've taken a loss, a heavy loss. But just as I made money for two years I can go on making money. It'd be easier if I could borrow more money—three thousand more. I'll repay it as I repaid the first two thousand dollars.'

'What if you have another fire?'

'I don't think I will.'

Matthews said, 'Are you asking for more money?'

'Yes. Three thousand, added to the thousand I still owe.'

'We can't do it. We can't make you another loan.'

'Why, Matthews?'

'It'd be too big a risk.'

'You mean there might be another fire.'

Matthews peaked his fingers together. He said, 'No, Carnaby, I wouldn't base everything on another fire. There are other things to consider. Outlaws raided your place. They might come again. In protecting your place you might be killed. Your place is almost out of the basin, too far away to be defended. I should never have approved your first loan. It's impossible to approve another. That's final, Carnaby. I'm sorry.'

'No loan,' Ben said quietly.

'No. Another loan is out of the question.' Matthews cleared his throat. 'What I really wanted to talk to you about was the money you still owe us—one thousand, one hundred and twenty-three dollars, and seventeen cents.'

Ben leaned forward. 'Wait a minute, Matthews. I signed up to repay the loan on a quarterly basis, plus interest. When is my next payment due?'

'August fifteenth.'

'And on that day I'll owe you two hundred and fifty dollars, plus interest.'

'That's right.'

'Today, right now, I don't have to pay the

40

bank a cent. Right?'

'Well, I suppose so . . .'

'Good,' Ben said, and stood up. 'Don't ask me for a nickel until August fifteenth.'

The man's lips tightened. 'I'll remember.'

'I'll bet you do,' Ben said, and he stepped outside, closed the door quietly, and left the bank. It might not have been easier to breathe outside but it seemed that way. He was mad, wanted to hit something. Of course he would get over that. Maybe, from the way Matthews looked at things, he was a bad risk. Maybe the banker was right.

He had missed his noon meal and it occurred to him that some steak, potatoes and gravy, topped off with coffee and pie, ought to make him feel a lot better. He needed something like that, with possibly a drink before he came to the food. Andy Thorne hadn't found him, as he'd promised. That might have been because he was still working on a bottle. With this in mind, Ben headed for the town's largest saloon, the El Monte.

He moved in that direction, wondering vaguely what he ought to try next. He had some money in the bank, about four hundred dollars, and he had just under two hundred dollars in the money belt he was wearing. That would keep him running, personally, for quite a while, but it wouldn't go far in rebuilding the ranch, or buying more horses. He needed the loan that Matthews had refused.

41

The El Monte was just ahead. He walked toward the bar, aware that the room was fairly well filled. There were eight or nine men at the bar, lounging there, drinking. There were more at the tables, some just sitting there, talking and drinking. At two tables games were in process. Ben looked around for Andy. He found him at a table with two other men, Carl Hughes and Milo Burke, who worked for Iron Kate. Remembering that Iron Kate wanted to see him, Ben briefly wondered if she'd loan him the money, but he was sure she wouldn't. She lived up to her name—Iron Kate.

Ed Yancy, who owned the place, was helping one of his bartenders. He noticed Ben, walked toward him and said, 'Tough what happened, Ben. Wish I could help you. Have one on the house, anyhow.'

He set a bottle of whiskey on the bar, pushed it forward. Then he set out a glass so Ben could pour what he wanted.

Ben took a generous drink, wondering if Yancy had ever done anything like this before. He was reputed to be a tight-fisted man. Yancy was about average in height, but thin, gaunt, round-shouldered. He had dark eyes under heavy brows and it seemed he always needed a shave. He kept a loaded shotgun under the edge of the bar and had been known to use it. Ben had never liked the man. When he had been serving as sheriff he had had trouble with him several times. So he was a little amazed at the man's attitude now.

He tasted the drink, then said, 'Thanks, Yancy.'

'Know what you're gonna do now?' the saloon owner asked.

'Start up again.'

'Just what I figured,' Yancy said.

He glanced toward the door, then stiffened, but for only a minute; his eyes hardened and then he looked away.

Ben decided it was worthwhile looking around. He did. And he was glad he did. The man who had caught Yancy's attention was Taft. Now that Ben had a good chance to observe the outlaw in the light, he could see that Taft was heavy, wide-shouldered, and he might have been in his late thirties. He had small, dark eyes, rounded cheeks. He started toward the bar, but stopped suddenly, his body stiffening. He was staring at Ben, must have recognized him.

It was noisy in the place, but not as noisy as it had been a few moments before. Several people nearby noticed Taft stopping short and the way he arched his arm so that his hand was close to his holstered gun. They stopped talking, moved back.

A man at the bar near Ben edged away, to where it might be safer. Yancy did the same thing. Ben didn't see that, but he sensed it. He was still staring at Taft and he hadn't spoken, but now he did. He called out, 'Taft! Where

43

are my horses?'

He half shouted the words. Everyone in the room heard him. The talking stopped. There was an almost hushed silence.

Taft didn't say a word, but after a moment Ben spoke again. 'Taft, I asked you a question. I'll ask it once more. Where are my horses?'

The man shook his head but he made no other answer. He had hunched over and suddenly, with no warning at all, he clawed at his gun, jerked it from its holster, started to lift it.

That was as far as he got. Ben moved more quickly. He whipped up his gun and fired it. He fired just once, but that was enough. His bullet hit Taft in the chest, driving him backward. He lost balance, crashed to the floor. He was still holding his gun, but he would never use it again.

Ben took a quick look around the room. Taft might have had friends in the place, but if he did they were keeping very quiet about it. For several moments no one spoke. Ed Yancy, back at the bar, had reached for his shotgun. He was just holding it, indicating he didn't want any more trouble in his place of business.

Someone else came barging into the room. It was Brazos Fowler. He was already holding his handgun, ready to use it, and he was breathing heavily as though he had been running. He came to an abrupt stop near Taft's body, looked down at him, then raised his head, scanning the room. Ben had holstered his gun.

'All right, who shot him?' Brazos asked.

'I did,' Ben said quietly.

'Then I'll take your gun,' Brazos said, and he stepped over Taft's body, starting forward.

'No, I don't think you will,' Ben said. He raised his gun casually. He was careful not to point it at the deputy, but in an instant he could have shifted aim.

Brazos stopped again. 'What the hell did you say?'

'Let me put it this way,' Ben said. 'You've got no reason to ask for my gun. Ask someone what happened. Ask anyone.'

One of the men in the room spoke up. 'He's right about that, Brazos. The man who got shot is the one who went for his gun. Any court in the land would call it self-defense.'

Another man spoke. 'That's the way it was, Brazos.'

Several more nodded.

Brazos seemed to hesitate. He called out, 'Yancy, what do you say?'

'It was like everyone else says,' Yancy replied. 'Didn't look like Carnaby's fault.'

The deputy stared at Ben, his eyes narrowed. He was tight-lipped. He didn't move them much when he spoke. 'What did you shoot the man for?'

'He reached for his gun,' Ben answered.

'What made him do that?'

45

'I asked him where my horses were. Taft was a horse thief. And if I can find his two friends I'll ask them the same question.'

'You sound pretty damn sure about it.'

'I'm the one who took the loss.'

'And your name is Carnaby?'

'Ben Carnaby.'

'Hm. I've heard about you, Carnaby,' Brazos growled. 'Maybe you can get out of it this time, claiming self-defense. Next time it might be different.'

IV

Ben finished his drink at the bar after Fowler left. Andy joined him. He'd been drinking but he seemed steady enough.

'Jeez, it sure happened fast,' he muttered. 'I didn't even see you come in.'

'That's all right,' Ben said. 'You hungry?'

'I guess I can eat. Wanna finish this drink, first.'

Ben had been steady when he fired the shot. Now, he was afraid he was a little shaky. His stomach was churning. He had another drink while Andy was finishing. More men arrived, to carry away Taft's body. One of the bartenders spread old newspapers where the blood had been.

Andy had a sudden thought. 'What if Taft's two friends are waiting outside?'

'Then there'll be more shooting,' Ben answered.

He had thought about that himself. He didn't want to step outside and run into a sudden attack. And it wasn't fair to Andy.

'Are you ready?' he asked bluntly.

'I guess so.'

'We'll leave by the back door,' Ben said. 'No reason not to play safe.'

The rear of the saloon could have been covered, too. Ben knew that, but he thought it

47

was their best chance. No one shot at them. There was a chance that Taft's companions were keeping out of sight.

Ben and Andy moved back to the plaza through one of the passageways between the buildings. There was only one restaurant. It was between the hotel and the stagecoach station. Sometimes the place was crowded, but this was before the supper hour and there were only a few other customers.

They took a table toward the rear, had coffee right away and ordered steaks, potatoes, gravy and bread.

Andy relaxed in his chair. 'One marked off,' he said. 'Two more to go. You're doing all right, Ben.'

'No, there might be more than two.' Ben shook his head. 'We don't know what we're up against. I didn't ask you this, myself, but who else in the basin has been hit by the outlaws?'

Andy scowled, shook his head. 'Can't think of anyone—but then I haven't gone around asking.'

'Suppose I was the only one who was raided.'

'Then I guess the raiders just swept through the basin—hardly stopped.'

'That isn't the way it usually is.'

'No, it's not. I wonder . . .'

Andy broke off, looked toward the door and Ben turned his head in that direction. A man had just come in. He was tall, heavily built and he stood quite straight. He had sand-colored hair, ruddy cheeks and a rather pleasant smile. He might have been in his thirties and he was walking toward them.

Andy touched his gun.

'Easy,' Ben said. 'Do you know him?'

'I think . . .'

The man reached them, pulled off his hat. 'My name's Kelly,' he said, smiling. 'Chico Kelly. Me and my partner have bought the Rowland place, so I guess we're neighbors. I wanted to meet you, Carnaby.'

'How did you know me?' Ben asked.

'I was in the saloon a few minutes ago.'

Ben nodded slowly. He motioned to the side. 'This is Andy Thorne, who works with me.'

'Howdy,' Andy said.

Chico nodded.

'Want to join us?' Ben suggested.

The man shook his head. 'No, I don't think a man ought to be troubled while he's eating, but I want to talk to you, sometime. Any chance you can stop at the ranch—the old Rowland ranch?'

'I might be able to make it.'

'Drop in anytime. I want you to meet Eddie Bryan—you'll like him. We might want to make you a proposition.'

'Propositions are always interesting,' Ben said.

'I'll count on seeing you, then?'

'That's right.'

The man nodded, turned, heading for the door.

'Now, what the hell does that mean?' Andy asked.

'How would I know?' Ben shrugged and watched the man step outside and head down the street.

'You gonna see him?'

'Why not? I wonder what he wants.'

'Me too,' Andy said. 'He's after something. People are always after something.'

Their steaks arrived and for the next few minutes there was no time to talk. It was a good steak. It had been weeks since Ben had enjoyed a meal like this. He took time with it. Andy got far ahead of him.

Ben was just finishing when Chico returned. By that time the restaurant had more customers, although it still wasn't crowded.

The man headed straight for their table, pulled out a chair and sat down without asking if he could. He spoke quickly, and in a low tone of voice. 'I don't want to butt into something that ain't my business, but there's two men at the corner of the building, watching the front door. They're near a passageway to the rear and there's two saddle horses tied back there. The two men are carrying rifles. Could be they're not interested in you, or maybe they are. I never saw them before.'

Ben nodded. He thought that the two men might have been Taft's companions. He said, 'Thanks, Chico. Do you know Brazos?'

'Saw him riding down the street a little while ago, heading out. Don't think he's come back.'

'Do you know Fred Gibbons?'

'I've met him.'

'Send someone after him. He's home. Most everyone knows where he lives. Get him to his office—that is—are you offering to help me?'

'That depends on what you want. If those two men are outlaws and if you want them under lock and key, then I'm your man.'

'Good. Think you can block the passageway? Do you have any of your men?'

'Two men. The three of us can block the passageway. But if you walk out on the street the shooting might start right away.'

'We'll go out the back way,' Ben said. 'Head to the third passageway, move back to the street and walk toward the restaurant. We might reach the men before they see us.'

'You'll have to move fast,' Chico said, and he stood up. 'Me, too.'

'We'll give you a five minutes start,' Ben said.

'Three minutes,' Chico said, and turned, heading for the door.

Ben looked at Andy. 'Want to stay with me?'

'Sure I do,' Andy said. 'But what are we getting into with Chico Kelly?'

'Nothing. He's helping us grab a couple of outlaws. That doesn't buy us.'

'I don't know,' Andy said uneasily. 'I guess I just don't like the man.'

Ben wondered why. Without really knowing Kelly he rather liked him. Chico made a good first impression.

'Time to go,' he said abruptly.

He stood up, left the money necessary for the meal on the table, and turned and headed for the kitchen. He could hear Andy following him. They went through the kitchen, nodded to the woman cook and the girl washing dishes, moved on to the back door and stepped outside. To the right was a passageway to the plaza and off to the side, back of the restaurant, were two horses, tied to the fence. They were saddled, ready to travel. Presumably they belonged to the two men up the passageway, watching the restaurant's front door.

Ben, with Andy following him, reached the passageway. Ben looked toward the plaza. Three men were grouped on the plaza street. Two might have been the outlaws, or a third might have been added. He would find out soon enough. Chico and his men were not yet here to block the passageway, but they might be on their way. Ben and Andy hurried on, past one building, then another, to the third passageway to the plaza. They moved back to the street, stopping briefly.

'Ready?' Ben asked, touching his holstered gun.

'What do we do?' Andy asked. 'Just move up on them, hope they don't see us?'

'That's about it,' Ben said, and he peered ahead.

This was a narrow building—the land office. Next was the stagecoach station; beyond was the restaurant. The two men waiting for him were at the far end of the station or across the passageway and in front of the edge of the restaurant. The three men he'd spotted earlier were still there, trailing their rifles. Three men were walking this way, two were headed in the other direction. Ben didn't think he knew any of them, but then he scarcely noticed them. It occurred to him that the waiting men might have just climbed from the coach. In this Indian country people often carried rifles when traveling. These men might have had nothing to do with Taft—but he would find out about that in a moment.

He passed the land office, aware that Andy was right with him. He moved on, started across the porch of the station house. One of the three waiting men turned his head, looking Ben's way. He stiffened instantly, and Ben nodded, recognizing him. The man was thin, hunched, had a gaunt, hungry look. Up there in the Ute Hills, he was the man who had run things, who had ordered Taft to dismount and move around behind him. The other two men . . .

Ben whipped out his gun, leveled it. The man looking his way called out a warning and started to swing his rifle. One of the other men looked Ben's way—and stiffened. The third man dived for the passageway, disappearing from sight. Ben could have dropped him, but presumably Chico Kelly and two of his men would be waiting at the other end of the passageway.

'Stand where you are,' Ben ordered. 'Drop your rifles. Now!'

Both dropped their rifles. The hunched man had nothing to say, but the one Ben didn't know did some quick thinking, and asked angrily, 'What the hell is this all about? What've we done?'

'If you don't know, I'm sure sorry,' Ben answered. 'Go get their rifles, Andy.'

A tense crowd was gathering. Andy got the two rifles, backed away. There were sounds from the passageway. The one who had tried to escape returned to join the other two. He'd been stopped by Chico Kelly and two of his men.

'We just got there in time,' Chico said, and he seemed to be enjoying himself. 'Sent word to Fred Gibbons. What do we do—march these men to the jail?'

'That's about it, Chico,' Ben answered. 'Many thanks.'

The three men headed toward the jail under

the guns of Ben, Andy, Chico and two of his men, Sam Niles and Ray Osborne. A score of others trailed along. Fred Gibbons wasn't at his office, but he got there a few minutes later, and he promptly put the three men in jail. They gave their names as Mark Quigley, Pancho Cos, and Lou Jerrod, and they claimed they'd done nothing wrong. Ben charged them as horse thieves.

'You got to be able to prove this,' Gibbons said, scowling.

Ben nodded. 'I know. I'll talk to the judge.'

'He's holding court in Tucson. Won't be back until next week.'

'I'll talk to him then; keep the three men in jail.'

'Guess I can do that,' Gibbons said.

Ben turned away. He thanked Chico again for his help, promised to see him, then he rejoined Andy, who was waiting outside the sheriff's office. Most of the crowd that had followed them to the jail had wandered away.

Andy was scowling. He shook his head, didn't seem at all elated about what happened. 'Did you notice those two men with Chico Kelly?'

'Sam Niles and Ray Osborne?' Ben nodded. 'They looked like two good men.'

'Gunhands,' Andy said. 'Did you notice how low their holsters were tied? How they handled their irons? I wouldn't want to go against them.'

Ben frowned. 'Most men are fair to good with their guns. If you've got to use a gun, you might as well be one of the best. What's eating at you?'

'Trouble.'

'Trouble in the basin?'

'It's coming, Ben. I can smell it in the air. Here's a rifle you might need.' He held it out. 'I saved it from one of the men we arrested.'

'Thanks,' Ben said, grinning. 'I'll borrow it. Ready to ride out?'

'Where?'

'Down the basin. We'll sleep out, drop in on Iron Kate for breakfast.'

'We could stay in town,' Andy said. 'I'm a little behind on my drinking.'

'And that could lead to trouble,' Ben said. 'We'll ride.'

They headed for the livery stable. Ben waited there while Andy headed to the store to buy blankets for a bedroll for Ben, a slicker in case of rain, some rifle shells and coffee. Andy traveled with a coffeepot in his saddlebags.

Ackerman had a horse ready for Ben and a loan saddle. He looked at Ben and chuckled. 'You been cutting up, from what I've heard— even put a check-rein on our deputy. That's something folks don't do. Where you and Andy headed?'

'Down the basin?'

'That's the way Brazos rode. There's a good many places along that river road where a man

56

could wait, and never be seen.'

'You mean I ought to head across country?'

'No reason you shouldn't. Remember where I turned in once, with a bottle? I dropped out of sight for three days—and all the time I was back in my baled hay. Had sort of a nest. You finally found me. That was when you was acting sheriff.'

'I remember the place,' Ben said, nodding.

'It's still there—a good hideout in case you need it.'

'Thanks, Rod.' Ben meant it. 'I hope I never need it, but it's good to know I can use it.'

Andy showed up with the things he had gone after and a few minutes after that he and Ben left town, heading down the valley. But a mile out of town, Ben cut away from the road and slanted across the range, pointing to the east.

'If we're headed for Iron Kate's, the road would be easier,' Andy said.

Ben shrugged. 'I want to look over the country.'

'Then if we're headed this way, in another mile we'll come to the Mexican town on Chaparral Creek. There's a cantina there . . .'

'You can go there another time,' Ben said, grinning. 'Just out of curiosity, how many bottles have you got in your saddlebags?'

The man laughed. 'Just a couple—in case of snakebite.'

'Then two bottles is enough,' Ben said.

*   *   *

They camped for the night in the scanty trees bordering Miser Creek, getting up early the next morning while it was still dark. They took time for coffee, then rode on, heading now to the north. They came in sight of the Salter Ranch. The place looked just like it did when Ben had worked there. There was the main house and, beyond it, three cabins for the men. Ben had had one of the cabins to himself while he had been there. He thought Dave Eckert had it now. There was a barn, a shed, three outhouses and a corral. Across the garden and away from the prevailing winds was a pigsty. The chickenyard adjoined the barn.

Smoke was coming from the chimney of the house and when Ben and Andy rode into the yard, Ben called, 'Hello, Kate! How about a handout for two hungry men?'

The door opened almost at once and Kate stepped out on the porch. She was tall, thin, but hard-muscled. She could outride many a man and was good with a rope. She might even have been good with the gun she wore, but Ben had never seen her use it. She had gray hair, twisted and knotted on her head; her face was leathery. She had thin, tight lips, cold blue eyes, flat cheeks. She stood very straight. He had never seen her smile. Maybe she could but he doubted it. Usually she seemed mad. And usually she dressed just like she did now, in boots, a worn pair of levis, faded blue shirt and a man's dark coat.

'Huh!' She cleared her throat. 'You could have come last night.'

'I'm used to sleeping out,' Ben answered.

'Tie your horse and come on in. You too, Andy Thorne.'

'Thanks, Kate,' Ben wheeled away, rode to the corral fence, dismounted, tied his horse. He ignored Kate's curt attitude; he always had. He had decided that was the only way to treat her.

Andy followed him. He dismounted, but under his breath he said, 'Hell with her. Don't know why we ever came here.'

They went inside. Dave Eckert, Carl Hughes and Milo Burke were still at the breakfast table. These three men represented Kate's crew. She was the foreman, rode with them. Dave had been here when Ben worked here before; the other men were new.

They had about finished breakfast and they soon left, except Dave, who served as host. Kate did the cooking, then she joined them at the table, having more coffee.

Andy had nothing to say. He ate, and listened. Ben asked about rustling but Dave said the basin had not been bothered by that for several years. 'That's not counting the raid on your place,' he said. 'Could be the men who hit your place wanted horses, not cattle.'

'I came back with a string of mustang mares,' Ben said slowly. 'The day I got here three men jumped me, knocked me out and took the mares. A few miles from the ranch they set them free.'

'That don't make sense,' Dave said, frowning.

'Met one in town yesterday afternoon,' Ben said. 'You might have left town before then. I asked the man what happened to my horses. He went after his gun.'

'Did you get him?'

Ben nodded. 'That took care of one of the outlaws. A little later on, with the help of Chico Kelly, we picked up three more. Fred Gibbons put them in jail.'

Kate leaned forward. Her voice was sharp. 'What did you say, Ben?'

'We put them in jail.'

'No. You mentioned Chico Kelly.'

'Yes, he helped me, he and two of his men.'

'Huh! Hard to believe that,' Kate said. 'It don't fit. Something wrong with it.'

'Maybe not,' Dave said.

'What do you mean?'

'If we're headed for trouble here in the basin maybe Chico wanted to look good—to the people in town. He helped to round up three outlaws. That puts him on the right side of the law. What folks won't see is the way he gets the outlaws free.'

'Huh! Maybe you're right.' Kate got up,

poured more coffee for them all.

'You mean the three outlaws won't stay in jail?' Ben said.

'That's my guess,' Dave said. 'I'd even bet a few dollars that I'm right.'

'And how about Chico Kelly?'

Dave looked at Kate. 'You tell him.'

'That's what I wanted to see Ben about,' Kate said, and she settled down in her chair. 'Ben, I hope you haven't made any deals with those two Texans.'

'I've made no deals with anyone,' Ben answered.

'Good. That's where the trouble's coming from—across the river. And not from Jeff Lorimer.'

'Trouble? What kind of trouble?'

'Bad trouble. Do you want to know what's happened in Cougar Basin? Not much that you can see on the surface. Harry Rowland sold his ranch. It was bought by two Texans, Chico Kelly and Eddie Bryan. They took over everything Rowland had, except his wife, and she was never his, anyhow. She belonged to Jeff Lorimer.'

Kate paused, frowned, took a taste of the coffee.

'You could have left Jeff out of it,' Dave said.

'Why should I?' Kate shook her head. 'Could be he planned the whole thing. Could be he thought Harry would take the money, and leave his wife behind. Jeff's a man you can never trust.'

'You're getting away from the Texans,' Dave said.

'I'll get back to them,' Kate said. 'Those two Texans moved in with maybe five or six hundred head of cattle. Harry had about a thousand. Fifteen, sixteen hundred head of cattle is about all that can be grazed on the land he owns, but do you know what's gonna happen? Those two Texans own twenty-five hundred more cattle—and they're on their way here now. What do you think is gonna happen when they get here? Can't you just see it—four thousand head of cattle on the Rowland range. Where can they put them?'

'Four thousand head,' Ben said, shaking his head. 'That's too many. If they had most of Jeff's land . . .'

'All right, let them move that way—south.' Kate was being very definite. 'Let them move in on Lorimer. Who cares about him, anyhow? Around here there's only one rule—we hold the line at the river. Any Texan cow found on our land gets shot.'

Ben was silent. He was thinking about what Kate had said about the Texans. If they were already grazing fifteen hundred head of cattle on the Rowland range, that was almost too many. If more were coming, then they faced a serious problem. Where could they be grazed? A few might drift north, into the Ute Hills, but they could be lost. There was not much grass, anyhow. The trees were too thick. To the west of the Rowland range the land turned bad. To the south was Lorimer's range, to the east was the river—and the land belonging to Iron Kate Salter. If Iron Kate held the line at the river, then any extra cattle would have to move south, spill into Jeff Lorimer's range.

'Ben, you're in trouble, too,' Kate said. 'The outlaws didn't leave you much, did they?'

'The land,' Ben answered.

'And you're still in debt to the bank. If the land would pay your debt, where does that leave you?'

'Sort of at the beginning.'

'Want some money?'

'A loan.'

'Two thousand?'

'Three.'

'All right, three. Three thousand dollars, at ten percent interest,' Kate said. 'I'll cancel the interest for three months of work on the Salter ranch. Take it or leave it.'

'Just like that, huh?'

'Just like that.'

'I want to think about it.'

'Sure,' Kate said. 'Go ahead. Think about it.'

V

The proposition had come suddenly, but then Ben knew that he should have expected it, just like that—in blunt, hard terms, and in full view of the problems he faced. If he stayed here for three months he would be expected to hold the line at the river, against any invasion. He would get help, whatever he could stir up. Kate would fight for her land, and he could count on Dave Eckert. Andy might stay, but he wasn't sure about the other two men working here. Both might leave.

'I ain't gonna stay here,' Andy said. 'Count me out.'

'I haven't said what I'd do,' Ben said quietly.

'Did you talk to Matthews?'

'He said no.'

Kate broke in. 'I was counting on that. Knew what Matthews would say. He plays safe. And he never liked you, Ben. You married Opal Lorimer. He had things fixed up so that his son would marry her. She might have been able to straighten him up.'

'Hank Matthews? What's happened to him?'

'Nothing. He hangs around town, lapping up liquor, sleeping with one of Laura's girls when he's got the money. He's no damn good.'

Ben recalled, 'While I was acting sheriff I

picked up Hank Matthews several times. He had a habit of drinking too much. Several times I put him in jail to sober up. His father thought I should have taken him home.'

'He's not worth talking about,' Kate said.

'Did you hear me?' Andy said. 'I'm moving out.'

'I heard you,' Ben said. 'But don't push me. Matthews said no to a loan. I don't think I can change his mind. In face of that I can do one of two things: make a loan somewhere so I can rebuild my ranch. Or I can turn it back to the bank, to satisfy the loan against it.'

'I don't sell myself,' Andy said. He glared at the table, didn't look up.

Kate's voice was sharp. 'Who cares about you? We can get along without you.'

'No, you're wrong, Kate,' Ben said. 'If what you've told me is true, you need every man you can get. How about Hughes and Burke?'

'They'll stay with us,' Kate said.

'They might stay,' Dave corrected her. 'We don't know how bad this might be.'

'How do you know the Texans are moving in more cattle?'

'George Matthews told Kate about the new cattle. Tell him, Kate.'

Her frown was deeper. Her voice was even sharper. 'That Matthews! He had the nerve to ask if I wanted to sell part of my range—said I didn't need so much land—but to hell with him.'

'Did he say the Texans were bringing in twenty-five hundred head?'

'That's what he said.'

'When do they get here?'

'They're due here now. We've got no extra time, Ben. In any minute we might be up to our necks in trouble.'

Ben nodded. He got up, walked to the window and looked out. The two new men, Carl Hughes and Milo Burke, had saddled up and were standing near their horses, at the corral fence. Hughes was the taller of the two, thinner, younger. Milo Burke was about as average in appearance as a man could be. Ben wondered how long the men might stay, then he wondered if he was even considering Kate's proposition. Did he want to stay here? No. But he needed three thousand dollars and here was a way to insure a loan of the money. Where else could he get it. Nowhere else. The average man around here didn't have that kind of money, or if he did he hung onto it.

He spoke without turning around. 'Kate, I want the three thousand dollars in cash handed over to me. I'll sign an agreement to work for you for three months, my wages to cover the interest on the loan for three years. And I'll sign the loan papers.'

'No.' She snapped the word at him.

'Then there's no deal.'

'Three thousand dollars, now? You're crazy. I never heard of such a thing.'

'Forget about it, then.'

'If you got the money in cash, what would you do with it? Lose it somewhere?'

'That would be my problem.'

'Never. You get the loan in three months.'

'No, I want it now—in cash.'

'No.'

'Then that's that, Kate.' He turned and grinned. 'It was a good breakfast. You're a wonderful cook.'

'And you're a wonderful nothing.'

'You might be right, Kate.' Ben glanced at Andy. 'Let's move out.'

'That suits me perfectly,' Andy said, and he stood up, headed for the door.

Ben followed him. They went outside, stepped down from the porch, crossing toward their horses.

Dave Eckert, who had followed them, said, 'Ben, I'm sorry. Wish you could have stayed here. We've got a hell of a problem facing us. Don't know what we'll do when the Texans start pushing their cattle across the river.'

'Yep. It's a tough problem,' Ben said.

'What'll you be doing?'

'Don't know. I might even go fishing.'

'The Texans are bringing in more men. That's what they say.'

'They probably need them,' Ben said.

He untied his horse, swung into the saddle. Andy had already mounted. Kate came out on the porch, stared at them.

'All right, Ben.' Kate raised her voice. 'You win. You get the money in cash. We need you.'

He reined up. He was surprised at Kate's decision, and it ran through his head that there was a trick in this somewhere. He called, 'Three thousand in cash, delivered to my hand.'

'That's what I said.' Kate nodded. 'Sign the loan paper and the agreement to work here for three months, your wages to cover the interest for three years.'

Andy had stopped, turned back, but he was scowling, shaking his head. He didn't seem to like this at all.

Ben looked at Kate. 'When do I get the money?'

'Tomorrow. Could be tonight.'

'Want me to draw a line at the river?'

'I expect you to.'

'I'll need more men.'

'Hire them.'

'Dave, how do you feel about this?'

The man didn't hesitate for a moment. 'I'll ride with you, Ben. We won't have any trouble.'

Ben turned back to Andy. 'How about you?'

'Hell with her,' Andy said. 'I'm pulling out.'

'What'll you do?'

'Don't know. It won't be hard getting a job. I'll hang around town for a while, see what shows up. Don't worry. I'll be seeing you, Ben.'

The man turned away, rode off. Ben

watched him for a time. He was sorry to see Andy go.

*　　　　*　　　　*

Later that morning, Kate sent Carl Hughes off on an errand. Then she announced she wanted to go to town and wanted Dave to go with her. Ben had no objections. Maybe the trip to town was to pick up his three thousand dollars. With three of them gone he had only one man to worry about, Milo Burke. If anything important had to be done, maybe he could handle it. Ben asked Dave what had been planned for the day.

'Nothing much,' Dave answered. 'We've been letting things slide so we could ride the river. Maybe you'd like to do that—take a look at where our trouble's coming from.'

'I'll find something to do, anyhow,' Ben said.

'Want the cabin you used to have?'

'No. Any bunk's all right. Three months isn't long.'

Dave Eckert was scowling. He said, 'Ben, those cattle are really coming, and when they get here they're gonna have to have grass. They're gonna have to have it right away. We won't have time to talk about it. Almost right away, somebody's got to give—Jeff Lorimer or Kate. And it won't be Kate. That's why you're here.'

69

Ben shrugged. 'It's already been spelled out for me, Dave. I know what's ahead—kind of a war.'

'Ever been through one?'

'No.'

'I went through one. It was godawful. Some damn good people got smashed. Even those who came out on top paid for it. If there was any way to stop it . . .'

'How could we stop it?' Ben asked.

'That's the trouble—I don't know. But think about it. Maybe you can figure out something I ain't seen. If it's there, go after it, no matter what Kate says.'

'Thanks, Dave.'

'I'll do anything I can,' Dave said, and he turned away.

Ben watched the man as he headed toward his cabin, a big man who moved slowly, deliberately. He had gray hair, might have been fifty. He was alone now, but he had been married once, had raised a family, then something had happened. He seldom referred to his earlier life. He had been with Kate for more than six years. He seemed to respect her—maybe he even loved her. At least he had stayed with her, seemingly unaware of her harshness.

Ben thought he was sure of one thing—he could count on Dave Eckert's help, no matter what happened.

Hughes had already left on his errand and a

few minutes later, Kate and Dave Eckert headed for town. Milo Burke looked at Ben and asked, 'What do we do this morning?'

'What did you do yesterday?' Ben countered.

'Rode the river.'

'What's happening to Kate's cattle, the east drift fences, the high land waterholes?'

'Guess we'll worry about things like that some other time.'

'What's going to happen when the Texas cows move in?'

'I guess you know more about that than I do.'

'Will you stay?'

'Might. I'm sort of tired of drifting. Up to now the work hasn't been too bad. 'Course I don't know what's ahead.'

'What is Kate paying you? Thirty dollars?'

'Yep. That's it. The day the Texas cows show up the pay doubles. If there's any shooting, we get five a day. I'll probably stay as long as I figure I can stay alive. If it looks like things are going to hell I'll have to move on. I'd sort of like to stay alive. How about you?'

'Sure, I'd like to stick around, grow bald, but I might never make it. Play as safe as you can, but your chances won't be any better. A friend of mine left the West because it was too dangerous to stay. The night he got back to Boston some waterfront tough put a knife in his back.'

Milo grinned. 'So I might as well stay here, huh? Let's see what happens. Do we ride the river?'

'Part of it,' Ben said.

They rode west to the river, following its course for several miles. Across the river were several small herds, belonging to Lorimer. In about an hour they came to the corner of the Rowland ranch. A wire fence, running west from the river, separated Lorimer's ranch from Rowland's. It was starting there, and on north, where he would have to hold the line against the Texas cows. They weren't yet there. There were only a few small herds of cattle on the Texans' ranch.

'No trouble yet,' Milo said, and he motioned to the trees and shrubbery along the river. 'We could hide an army on this river—if we had an army.'

'Sure, but if there were four thousand cows over there, parched for thirst, they'd roll right over the army. Ever been in a stampede? A push for water is just like it.'

'Then how do we hold the line?'

'We don't—not with our guns. We bluff it as far as we can, but when the cattle pile up and start smelling the water, then we drop the bluff and get out of the way.'

'Kate won't like it.'

'I know she won't,' Ben said. 'Want to visit the enemy?'

'If you do.'

'Then let's go see the Texans,' Ben said.

They forded the river, came to the valley road and crossed it. Beyond it was the Rowland range, now owned by the two Texans. Ben checked his handgun and he noticed Milo doing the same thing. He rather liked the man.

'I took a look at my handgun,' Ben said. 'But that's a habit. I don't think we'll run into any trouble. I met Chico Kelly—rather liked him.'

'Dave liked him,' Milo said. 'But I don't think he said that to Kate. He sort of—looks after her.'

Ben nodded. Maybe that outlined Dave's attitude toward Kate. He was a protector.

They passed more cattle, came finally in sight of the ranch buildings. It wasn't a large place, about the size of Kate's. If Kelly and Bryan were both married they were going to have to enlarge the main house, or build another. Ben noticed two men working in the yard, and someone came out of the house, a woman. She wore a pink dress. He was too far away to see her clearly but he sensed she was young.

As they rode nearer, the two men in the yard stopped working, and the woman went back into the house. The man who had been in the shade, mending harness, got up and went to the barn. He came out with his rifle. The other man, who had been chopping wood, put his ax aside and stepped to where his rifle was standing against a pile of wood.

'They're just edgy,' Ben suggested. 'Don't stiffen up.'

'I ain't stiffened up, yet,' Milo said.

They rode into the yard, reined up. The two men in the yard had separated, and now raised their rifles. One man was covering Ben, the other was covering Milo.

'This is a hell of a way to greet a man,' Ben said quietly.

The man who was covering Milo answered, 'What do you want?'

'I came to see Chico Kelly,' Ben said.

'He ain't here.'

'Where is he?'

'Don't know.'

'When'll he be back?'

'Don't know. Want to head out of here?'

The door to the house opened again and the woman came out. She wasn't as young as Ben had thought. But she was a rather attractive woman, probably in her early thirties, with piled up dark hair. She was carrying a rifle.

'I'm Mrs. Kelly,' she said. Her voice was a little sharp. 'What did you want with my husband?'

'Just wanted to see him,' Ben said. 'I met him in town. In fact, he helped me with three outlaws. My name is Carnaby.'

Her rifle had been half lifted but now she lowered it. 'Ben Carnaby? He mentioned you.

I'm sorry, he's not here. We've been expecting some cattle. There's some coming in on the south trail to the basin. Chico rode in that direction. I'm not sure when he'll be back.'

'Then I'll see him another time.'

She hesitated, then spoke quickly. 'Mr. Carnaby, the reason we greeted you like this was—was on account of what happened last night. Several men rode past. They came by quite late and they poured shots at the ranch. It's a miracle no one was hurt.'

Ben frowned. A night raid! Men riding by, pouring shots into the house! Who would do a thing like that? What did it accomplish? It could only tighten the tensions in the valley. It would lead to trouble before the issues were even defined.

'I'm sorry about what happened last night,' he said slowly. 'It shouldn't have happened. I wish I knew who was responsible, but I don't. If your husband was here . . .'

'Can you come back, Mr. Carnaby?'

'Yes, I'll be back when I can.' He was puzzling about what had happened. 'Tell your husband I want to see him; say that I'm working for Kate Salter, will you?'

'Kate Salter!' The woman straightened and her voice changed, hardened. It was evident she had heard about Kate and didn't like her. But she said, 'I'll tell my husband.'

Ben nodded, touching his hat, then he and Milo headed out of the yard. He was conscious

75

of the two men in the yard still covering them, but he didn't look directly at either one.

East of the house he spoke to Milo. 'From here we head south, and a little east.'

'To the Lorimer ranch?' Milo guessed.

'That's right.'

'At least I'm gonna earn my money if I ride with you,' Milo said.

'Why? Nothing happened at the Texans' ranch.'

'We had a few damned uncomfortable minutes. I don't like being gun-covered. What's gonna happen at Lorimer's?'

Ben shook his head. 'How would I know?'

'Do you get along with him?'

'Not too well.'

'Do you think he could've led the raid last night?'

'I hope not,' Ben said.

He was frowning. He meant what he said. He hoped Jeff Lorimer hadn't been responsible for the raid on the Texans' ranch, but he might have. Jeff was inclined to follow his impulses; he nearly always played a hunch. He seldom thought things out clearly, and he never seemed to learn from his mistakes. He was stubborn, opinionated but erratic. Those three characteristics, put together, resulted in a man hard to understand.

It was a fair trip over to the river and up the line, then across to the Texans' ranch and, after that, a drop to Lorimer's. The sun had moved into the western sky. It was afternoon, another day without dinner. Ben thought it was getting to be a bad habit.

Ahead of them now was the Lorimer ranch, the main house larger than Kate's. The barn was bigger and there was a good sized bunkhouse, two sheds, a larger corral and five outhouses. Ben decided that if a man's importance could be determined by the number of outhouses he needed, then Lorimer stood at the top of the list.

They rode into the yard, pulled up. Three men came into sight, not to gun-cover them, but their handguns were ready for trouble if they were needed.

Milo noticed where the three men were stationed. He spoke under his breath. 'We're boxed—if there's any trouble.'

'There won't be,' Ben said, and he raised his voice. 'Is Jeff anywhere around?'

'He's inside, I think,' someone said.

The man was right. Jeff came out on the porch, stopped, and stared at Ben. His lips were tight—there was no smile on his face—a tall, heavy-set man holding back the edge of his temper.

'Hello, Jeff,' Ben said.

The man glared at him. 'What the hell do you want?'

'I thought we might talk.'

'They tell me you went back to Iron Kate.'

Ben wondered how Lorimer had learned

77

about him so quickly, but then figured Kate might have talked in town, and one of Lorimer's men might have been there.

He said, 'Yes, I'm back at Kate's.'

'Then keep away from here.'

'Mostly, I will,' Ben said. 'But right now I think we ought to have a talk. You and me . . . or if you don't want to talk to me, talk to Kate. We're facing the same problem.'

The man shook his head. 'I don't know about you and Kate—and I don't care. If I'm facing any problems, I'll take care of them myself. And to hell with you.'

'What'll you do when the Texas cows get here?'

'They can move right in on you. They won't settle on my land. And that's a promise.'

'If we worked together . . .'

'With you? Or with that woman across the river? Never! Hell with both of you. You left here once. Wish you'd never come back.'

Ben sat there in the yard, wondering what he should say next, but he didn't know what would help. It had been a mistake to come here. Even in the face of the crisis that was ahead Lorimer wouldn't talk to him; his hatred hadn't lessened. It could be that he might have made some agreement with the Texans, Ben thought, an agreement to help push the new cows over the river and onto Kate's range. The man had never liked Kate, and this was a good way to hurt her.

78

One argument stood against such an agreement. If Jeff was going to help push the cattle onto Kate's range, he wouldn't have raided the Texans' ranch. Of course he might not have been responsible for the raid. It was just a guess that he had planned it.

Jeff spoke suddenly. 'I've spent too much time gabbing. Get the hell off my land, Ben. And don't come back.'

'I still think we ought to talk about what's facing us,' Ben said stubbornly.

'Hell with you! Get moving.'

Ben hesitated, but then shrugged and reached for the reins, turned his horse away, heading east.

Milo followed him, and when they were out of the yard the man spoke. 'Two of the men in the yard were itching to try their guns. You had me sweating. Let's get out of here.'

'We're moving fast enough,' Ben answered.

'How's Jeff Lorimer gonna keep the Texas cows off his land?'

'Make a guess, Milo?'

'He's got an army somewhere.'

'You and your army,' Ben said. 'An army won't do it.'

'He could try it.'

Ben shook his head. He doubted that Jeff had hired any extra men and, if he was right about that, then how would the man protect his range? The only thing he could think of was an agreement with the Texans. When the

79

cattle got here they would need more grass. There were only two ways they could drift— south onto Jeff's land, or east onto Kate's range. They wouldn't disappear and they wouldn't stand still.

'Dog eat dog,' Milo said.

'Looks that way,' Ben said. 'And I don't like it; not a bit.'

VI

There was no one outside in the yard when Ben and Milo got back to the ranch, but smoke showed from the house chimney, an indication that Kate and Dave had returned from town. Ben reined up in front of the barn, dismounted.

'Want me to look after your horse?' Milo asked.

'No, I'll take care of him later,' Ben said. 'Tie him to the corral fence. I want to see Kate.'

He headed straight for the house, went inside, heard someone in the kitchen and moved that way. 'Kate,' he called ahead, 'I wanted to ask you if . . .'

He reached the kitchen, looked in and saw a woman standing at the stove, stirring something in a pan, but it wasn't Kate. It was Tish Wellington. She was wearing a divided skirt and a white blouse, the sleeves rolled up over her tanned arms. Her hair was tightly pinned up and there was good color in her face as she looked toward him.

She said, 'Hello, Ben. There's lemonade over there.' She pointed across the room.

He stood just inside the room. 'What in the world are you doing?'

'Starting supper.'

'But how come?'

'Kate sent for me. She asked me several days ago if I could work for her. She wants to be able to work outside, needed someone to handle the inside chores. Any reason I shouldn't make the money?'

'Did Carl Hughes go after you?'

She nodded.

'What will your folks do while you're away?'

'Miss me. But they'll get along without me.'

'I hope you get your money,' Ben said bluntly.

'Now, that wasn't nice at all,' Tish said. 'Tonight you'll get burned potatoes.'

'I'll send them back.'

'Then you'll go without.' She frowned. 'What's going to happen, Ben? Carl told me about the new cattle that are on the way. What are they going to do?'

'I don't know, Tish. I wish I did.'

'What are those two Texans like—the new men who bought the Rowland property?'

'I've only met one,' Ben said. 'Chico Kelly. I rather liked him.'

'Doesn't he know he doesn't have enough pasture to look after more cattle?'

'He looks like a savvy man. He knows.'

'Then why is he bringing in more cattle?'

'Maybe he thinks someone will give him, or sell him, more land.'

'Kate won't. What about Jeff Lorimer?'

'He says no.'

The girl hesitated, then she said, 'Ben, is there any chance they might crowd the extra cattle to Red Mesa?'

'I hadn't thought about that,' Ben answered. 'There's enough land on the mesa, but not enough water. No, I don't think they'll push the cattle that way.'

'Then what will happen?'

'We're back to the original question. I still don't know. Did you bring your horse?'

'Big Red?' Her eyes brightened. 'He's in the barn. I want you to try him.'

'I'd want to keep him,' Ben said.

'Over my body,' Tish said. Then, when Ben just grinned at her, her cheeks showed extra color and she turned back to the stove.

'Maybe I'd better get out of here,' Ben said.

'No. Get your lemonade,' Tish said. 'But don't say anything cute or I'll start throwing things.'

Ben had his lemonade. It was cool and tart, not too sweet. In spite of what he had said at breakfast, Iron Kate wasn't a very good cook. Tish might be better. She was certainly easier to look at.

*   *   *

Within an hour, Kate and Dave returned from town. Kate had brought his money, three thousand dollars. It was in gold coin, in a leather pouch, and it was amazing how little space it took. Kate had also brought two papers for him to sign. One covered his loan, interest free for three years. The other paper was a pledge to work for Kate for the next three months, at no salary. Ben signed both papers and took the money.

Dave had news for him. It wasn't surprising. There'd been a jailbreak last night. It had been made late at night. Gibbons, who'd been alone in his office, had been struck over the head. He was still unconscious, might never wake up. Two drunks who had been in the jail, and the three outlaws, had escaped. The outlaws, apparently, had fled toward the badlands, but it was a guess where they had gone.

Brazos Fowler, the deputy, had been out of town, somewhere. At least that was what he said. Dave Eckert suggested that maybe that wasn't true.

'Heard anything more about the new cattle?' Ben asked.

Dave shook his head.

'They're due here soon,' Ben said bluntly. 'Chico Kelly rode out today to see if he could meet them. Last night, raiders swept past the Texans' ranch house, poured bullets at the place.'

'Now who the hell would do that?' Dave asked.

'Jeff Lorimer,' Kate said, and she scowled at him. 'How do you happen to know about it?'

'I rode that way, talked to Chico's wife.

84

Then I went to see Jeff Lorimer.'

'I want you to keep away from Lorimer,' Kate said. 'And that's an order.'

Ben shook his head. 'We might as well look at the truth. We can't hold against hungry, thirsty cattle; neither can Jeff. We've got to talk—you and Lorimer and the Texans.'

Kate Salter was angry. She raised her voice. 'I've got nothing to say to Lorimer, and I got nothing to say to those two Texans. You ought to know that.'

Ben noticed that Tish was watching and listening from the kitchen door. He wondered what she was thinking.

'Couldn't hurt to do some talking,' Dave said.

Kate glared at him. 'You keep out of this.'

'How did the Texans happen to buy the Rowland place?' Ben asked.

'George Matthews arranged it,' Kate said. 'But I'm sure he didn't figure the Texans were bringing in extra cattle.'

'We might ask him,' Ben said. 'In fact, I think I will, tonight. If he arranged the sale he ought to have a part in whatever decisions we make. He might even set up the meeting.'

'What meeting?' Kate snapped.

'A meeting between us, the Texans, Jeff Lorimer and Matthews.'

'I'll go to no such meeting.'

'But you will, Kate,' Ben said flatly. 'If you want to save this ranch of yours you'll do several things you never did before.'

'It's a waste of time,' Kate said. 'I want that river line held. That's what you're supposed to do.'

'There's more to holding a line than to ride it,' Ben said. 'You ought to know that.'

He went outside, switched his saddle to another horse, wondering what he ought to do with his three thousand dollars while he went to town. After a moment he decided to leave the money with Tish. She might not want to look after his money, but if she had to, she would. And he could trust her. He was sure of that.

He had worked here before, and knew the house well. There were only two bedrooms. Kate used one. The other would be the girl's. He went inside. He could hear the two women talking in the kitchen. The men were outside. He hurried to the second bedroom.

Ben put the gold under her mattress, wrote a note and put it under her pillow. The note told her where the money had been left, asked her to look after it. In another few minutes Ben was outside again, ready now to head toward town.

He had a brief talk with Dave and the two other men and, as he was ready to leave, Tish came out, carrying something wrapped in newspaper.

'Your supper,' she said, walking toward him. 'It'll be after dark before you get to town. I want you to be careful; don't get into trouble.'

'I won't,' Ben said. 'And thanks for the supper.'

'I suppose you know Kate's furious at you.'

'That's the normal state around here,' Ben said. 'You'll get used to it.'

She shook her head. 'No, I don't think I will. I liked Red Mesa. There's not much water and the grass isn't very good but there's never been any fighting. That makes it a very special place. Good night, Ben.'

He was holding her package, but he waved to her. 'Good night, Tish. How about pancakes for breakfast?'

'They'll be ready.'

He waved again, then rode away, headed toward town.

*   *   *

He had been riding most of the day and didn't push himself as he rode south. The supper was good, three fat meat sandwiches. He wouldn't have to stop at the restaurant when he got to town. That was helpful. He could head directly to Matthews' home. In that way he might not run into Brazos. He was still uneasy about the man, worried about him. The man was dangerous.

It grew dark, and when it was impossible to watch the changing scenery, Ben started thinking of what had been happening. He was looking for some kind of pattern. A ruthless man might need only a toehold on a new range, then depend on his own power to get what he wanted. The Texans could use the Rowland range as a base, and from there they could bring in hundreds of more cattle—and men and guns to back them up. They could then spread out, take what they wanted at gunpoint.

Was that what was happening? If it was, talking wouldn't help. The Texans would take what they wanted. In the process, a lot of people might get hurt.

Ben scowled, and shook his head. He didn't want to think that this was what was ahead, but most likely it was. There were the two Texan ranchers; the outlaw Taft had come from Texas, and maybe his companions. And Brazos Fowler had come from Texas; he seemed to fit into the picture, a part of the general scheme.

The lights of the town showed up in the far-off distance. Ben rode a little faster. Maybe he was wasting time in riding to town to see Matthews, in the hope that in some way or other all the involved parties could get together and talk over what was a common problem. But it was either that, or a basin war.

He came finally to the edge of town, moved on in but avoided the main street and the plaza. He reined up in front of Matthews' house, dismounted and tied his horse to the gatepost. It was late, but there was lamplight at the edges of the curtained windows. Ben moved closer, stepped up on the porch, knocked on the door. He waited for a moment, then knocked again.

Someone came to the door, opened it a crack and asked, 'Who is it? What do you want?'

'Carnaby,' Ben said. 'I want to talk to you, Matthews.'

'At this hour?' The man sounded angry. 'See me tomorrow if you've got to, but it won't do any good.'

The door was still partly open. Ben put out his hands, and pushed, pushed harder. He stepped inside in spite of the pressure of Matthews' weight, and said, 'Stop it, Matthews. I said I wanted to talk to you.'

The man stepped back. He was pale, breathing hard, still angry. 'I should have brought my gun. You've got no right to force yourself into my house.'

'No, I don't,' Ben admitted. 'But we're running out of time. More cattle are on the way to the basin. There's no place to graze them. That means there's going to be trouble.'

'That's none of your business,' the banker said. 'Nor mine.'

'Nope, you're wrong,' Ben said, and he reached back and closed the door behind him. 'It's my business, and it's yours. It's mine because I'm working for Kate Salter and some of the cattle now headed this way might spill out on Kate's land. It's your business because you sold the Rowland property to the men who now own it—Chico Kelly and Eddie Bryan.'

'A sale is a sale,' Matthews snapped. 'That's all there is to it.'

'Nope, you're wrong again,' Ben answered. 'A sale might be a sale, and nothing else, but most sales are put into some kind of framework. There are conditions, specifications, lists of what's included, terms of payments, dates and qualifications. And even if that wasn't the case, you ought to be interested in preventing trouble in the basin, because that's good business for everyone.'

'I don't need you to tell me what's good.'

'All right, I won't. Tell me about the sale of the Rowland range; what were the terms?'

Matthews raised his arm, pointed. 'Get out of here. You have no right to ask such a question.'

'Then let's talk about this,' Ben said. 'The Texans bought the Rowland range, and about six hundred head of Rowland's cattle. They added about a thousand head more. That chokes up the range. They can't add any more, but from what I heard twenty-five hundred more cattle are headed here. Now, tell me this. What's going to happen when they get here? Where will they graze, get water? I'd like to know.'

The man shook his head. 'I don't have to answer to you, Carnaby.'

90

'I think you do, because it touches me. Tell me, Matthews—when you sold the Rowland range to the Texans, did you know what they planned to do?'

'Of course not. I sold them land, that was all.'

'Then I want you to call a meeting of everyone concerned: Kate Salter, Jeff Lorimer, Kelly, Bryan, you and the sheriff.'

'Fred Gibbons is too sick to see anyone.'

'Then his deputy, Brazos Fowler. Call the meeting tomorrow.'

Matthews bit his lips. After a moment he shook his head. 'It's not up to me to call any meeting. I'll not do it.'

'Then get the mayor to call it. Do you want a war on your hands?'

'There's not going to be any war.'

'Where will they put the extra cattle? On whose range?'

'We never had any trouble before, just because someone brought in more cattle.'

'No one ever brought in so many, or tried to put them on such a narrow range.'

'They'll work it all out.'

'Who? That's what we're talking about.'

They were standing in the hall. There was a stairway to the second floor to Ben's left. The hallway extended to a door, probably to the kitchen. There were drawn curtains to the right, leading to the parlor, and now, suddenly, the curtains stirred. Someone was standing

91

there, out of sight, listening.

Ben dropped his hand to his gun. His voice tightened. 'Who's back of the curtains?'

'It's just me.' It was a woman who spoke. She parted the curtains enough so he could see her. It was Mrs. Matthews.

She was a tall, thin woman who stood very straight and whose appearance was usually asutere, forbidding, cold. Ben had the feeling she disapproved of nearly everything she saw. Tonight she seemed tense and angry.

'Don't worry, Mrs. Matthews,' he said, trying to reassure her. 'I'm just trying to get your husband to call a meeting which I think is necessary.'

He relaxed, dropped his hand from his gun. Mrs. Matthews moved again, moved further into the hall. She was holding a rifle. It had been hidden behind the curtain, but now, suddenly, it was out in the open and the woman lifted it, pointed it at him.

She was slow about it, and awkward. If it had been a man standing there, handling the rifle, Ben could have gunned him down. At least he could have handled her, but he didn't. He just looked at her.

By this time, Matthews had moved, reached into some pocket and drew out a derringer. He extended his arm toward Ben, the arm rigid, and he called out, 'Stand there where you are. Don't move or I'll kill you.'

From the way Matthews was acting, Ben

could see he had never done anything like this. He was not accustomed to violence. Because of that he was more dangerous. He might use his gun before he meant to.

Ben tried to speak quietly. 'I'm not going to move. I'm not threatening anyone. I just came here to talk to you. There's no reason to use your gun.'

The man didn't seem to listen. His body seemed frozen, his arm still extended straight toward Ben, the derringer pointed at his chest.

Matthews spoke again, in the same, high, excited voice. 'Move—and I'll kill you. Corithia, hurry downtown. Tell the first man you see to get Brazos Fowler. I want him out here right away.'

The woman lowered her rifle. She said, 'Yes, George,' and she edged past Ben, moved toward the front door. She didn't stop for a coat, or a bonnet. And she didn't close the door.

'I don't know why you're sending for Brazos,' Ben said, frowning. 'What are you going to tell him?'

'I'm going to have him put you in jail,' Matthew said. 'I'm going to keep you there.'

'Why?'

'You invaded my home. I won't stand for it.'

'All right, but this is a crisis. We're in trouble, on the edge of violence. You could do something about it—help put it off.'

'If there's going to be any trouble, you're

the one who's stirring it up.' The man nodded to himself. 'That's a good reason for keeping you in jail. When Brazos gets here . . .'

Ben tried to talk to him. He used every argument he could think of, but it seemed that Matthews had stopped thinking. He had fixed his mind on one thing—jail for Ben Carnaby.

VII

That was where Ben went—to jail. Brazos showed up with a tense, angry Mrs. Matthews, and a small and curious crowd of men. Ben was disarmed, then marched to the jail, and perhaps it was lucky the crowd was there. Brazos, in view of the curious who came to watch, had to act as an arresting officer, and deliver his prisoner.

The man had little to say at the Matthews' home, or on the way to jail, but when they got there and Ben had been locked in, Brazos could afford to make a few comments.

'You're damned lucky to get locked up,' the deputy said. 'If I had run into you on the street things might have worked out different.'

Ben looked at him curiously. 'Why?'

'You'd have gone after your gun, most likely—and you wouldn't have had a chance.'

'What's going to happen now?'

'Reckon you'll stay in jail.'

'How long?'

'Two or three days.'

'Why?'

The deputy shook his head. 'You ask too damn many questions.'

'I have more,' Ben said. 'Why am I here? What are the charges against me?'

'I guess that's up to Matthews.'

Ben glanced from side to side. He tested the barred door, then said, 'This hasn't been a very safe jail. I brought three men here. They didn't stay long.'

'They must have had friends,' Brazos said, and he laughed, wiped his hand over his face.

'So you're the one who let them out?' Ben said.

The man shook his head, but he still seemed amused. 'You're not the kind to last very long. Make a statement like that in town, and I'll blast you. I might even let you out, give you a chance to get at your gun. That would be a quick way to finish you.'

'Give me the chance now,' Ben snapped.

The man shook his head. 'Nope, we might need you.'

Ben was silent for a moment, thinking. What did Brazos mean? He had just said, *We might need you!* What did he mean by that, or more importantly, who did he mean by *we*? Who was included, and what were such men planning? He had been searching for a pattern to explain what was happening. He had seen a possible pattern in the Texans who had bought the Rowland range. This pattern was just a possibility, but from what Brazos had said, he knew the outlaws and had helped them break jail. The man had practically admitted it.

'I've got another question for you,' Ben said.

'I'm tired talking,' Brazos said, interrupting him. 'Got other things to do. Simmer down and shut up.'

He swung away, stepped into the front part of the sheriff's office and closed the door to the jail.

*   *   *

It was dark in the jail. It was smelly and the air was heavy. There was a wall bunk. Ben pulled it down, sat down on it, wondered how long he would have to stay here. If Iron Kate Salter found out what had happened to him, she'd move in a hurry, get him out of here no matter what she had to do.

He heard Brazos pacing the front office, heard him leave, slamming the door. Then, maybe an hour later, the man came back. He took a look into the jail, but he didn't say anything, then closed the jail door.

A little while later someone came in. Ben had no idea who it was. He could hear murmuring voices. Then there was another noise, a heavy, shaking sound and with a splintering of wood. He stood up, tensed, listening.

Two or three minutes passed, then the door opened and someone looked in at him. It wasn't Brazos, although the man was tall and thin as the deputy. The man's face was shaded from the light in the front office. It took Ben a moment to realize who it was—Hank Matthews, the banker's son. He was holding a handgun, just holding it, not pointing it, and he said, 'Ben . . .'

'Hank!' Ben was amazed. 'What are you doing here?'

'Thought you might want to get out,' Hank said. He was grinning. It wasn't a very good grin. He took time to look quickly over his shoulder into the office behind him.

'What happened?' Ben asked.

'I sort of used my gun on Brazos' head, while he wasn't looking. I had to hit him twice.'

Ben shook his head. It was hard to believe what Hank said. He wasn't the kind to take a desperate chance, or to get involved in anything like this. He was better in handling a bottle, or a woman. On several occasions he had tried to handle a job, but he'd never lasted very long.

'Hit him twice?' Ben said. 'But why?'

'After the first time he started to get up.' Hank looked back again. 'The second time I used a chair. I'm afraid I broke it.'

'And what do you think Brazos will do when he wakes up?'

'I don't expect to be here,' Hank answered.

'Where will you be?'

'With you—if you'll have me. At least that's what I want.'

'And what am I doing?' Ben asked.

'From what they say, you're working for Iron Kate, holding the line along the river against the Texans.'

'You want to try that?'

'Yes.'

'You don't know what you're talking about,' Ben said gruffly.

'Maybe not,' Hank said. 'But I think I do. In fact I've got to—I've got to show what I can do. You haven't said you want to get out.'

'I want to get out,' Ben said. 'If you've got the jail keys, use them.'

Hank had the keys. He holstered his gun, unlocked the cell door and Ben stepped outside, moved into the front office. Brazos had sprawled to the floor. He was lying unconscious, the broken chair partly on his body. There was an open wound on the side of his head, the result of Hank's first blow.

Ben found his handgun in the desk, made sure it was loaded, then holstered it. He glanced at Hank, who was watching him, and who asked suddenly, 'Do I go with you?'

'If you really want to,' Ben said.

'That's what I asked for. I've got two horses outside.'

'What if Brazos rides after you?'

'I don't think he will. Or if he does, I don't know what I'll do. Maybe that doesn't make much difference. We better get started, Ben. Someone could walk in anytime.'

Ben nodded, but he didn't start toward the door. He was still thinking about what might happen after Brazos woke up. The man would be furious about what had happened. It would be like him to head out after Hank Matthews and, if that happened, Hank wouldn't have a chance. Brazos was too good with his gun.

Ben looked down at him. The man was lying face-down, his right hand extended above his head, flat to the floor. Ben moved that way. He stepped on Brazos' hand, crushed the fingers, might have broken some of them. The man was not only going to have a headache, his right hand would be swollen, useless. It might be weeks before it was well again. He might be able to use his left hand, but he wouldn't be as dangerous as before.

Hank was waiting off to the side of the porch, pointed into the darkness. 'Our horses are over there.'

'Let's find them,' Ben said. 'Time to ride.'

*   *   *

Kate asked Ben to stay for a time after breakfast and Ben nodded, poured more coffee, then waited for the others to leave. That didn't take long. Carl, Milo and Hank moved outside as soon as they were through eating. Dave stayed long enough to offer to saddle Ben's horse.

Tish finished her last cup of coffee, then stood up and started clearing the table. She did this quietly, efficiently.

Kate, still at the table, frowned at her, then said, 'We won't have pancakes again. It's too much trouble.'

'We'll have pancakes when I feel like it,' Tish answered, smiling. 'Remember, you told me that the cooking was up to me.'

'I don't like pancakes,' Kate said.

'Then you can have bacon and eggs.'

Kate turned her attention to Ben. 'What did you accomplish in town?'

'Not much, probably.' Ben shrugged. 'I still think we ought to have a meeting, Matthews, the Texans, Jeff Lorimer and you. There might be a way to avoid trouble.'

'There's only two ways to avoid trouble,' Kate said sharply. 'One is for the Texans to turn the herds back. The other is up to Lorimer—let him give up half his range.'

Ben shook his head. 'He won't do that.'

'Then it's up to the Texans. Have them turn the herds back.'

'We can talk to them.'

'I'll do no begging,' Kate said sharply.

'Do you want a fight along the river? Do you want to see your men dead?'

'I don't think it'll come to that.'

'Nobody does. Everybody's looking the other way. Nobody is doing any thinking.'

'Was it sound thinking to hire a man like Hank Matthews?'

'What's the matter with him?'

'He's no good—never was—never will be.'

Ben shook his head. 'People change. Maybe Hank won't find what he wants here but if he's ever going to, he's got to get started. You wanted more men, anyhow. He adds up to one.'

'One we could get along without,' Kate said. 'I want you to ride the river—and that's all. I'm riding with you. Tish is fixing sandwiches.' The woman raised her voice. 'Tish, when will the sandwiches be ready?'

The girl had made several trips to the kitchen while they'd been talking, but now she was working there. After Kate called, she appeared in the doorway. 'The sandwiches are ready. I got up early and fixed them.'

'Good. Do that always.' Kate stood up, turned toward the bedrooms, but stopped suddenly and looked back at Ben. 'What are you waiting for?'

'More coffee,' Ben said.

The woman pointed at him. 'You leave Tish alone.'

'She's big enough to look after herself,' Ben said.

'There does happen to be more coffee,' Tish said, and she went to get it.

Kate shook her head, frowning at Ben. 'Leave her be,' she said, and moved on to her bedroom.

Tish brought him more coffee, then she spoke under her breath. 'You shouldn't have left your money with me. I won't be responsible for it. I want you to look after it yourself.'

'I can't very well today,' Ben said. 'I'll be riding to see the Texans. There might be trouble.'

'Then I want you to take it tonight. Why are you going to see the Texans?'

'I think we ought to talk. Didn't you hear what I said to Kate? We're heading into trouble, real trouble. There's no sense in it.'

'And talking will help?'

'It might. Men can always fight. But they can talk, too. They can reason, and if they try hard enough they can usually find a way around their problems.'

She spoke slowly. 'I'm just beginning to realize how stubborn Kate can be. If Jeff Lorimer is as bad as her, what chance do we have?'

'None, maybe,' Ben said, and he tried more coffee, sat scowling at the table.

'Some of the extra cattle could be put on the mesa, for a time,' Tish said. 'The grass isn't as good as in the basin and someone would have to dig more wells, but I think . . .'

'That's it,' Ben said. 'You're starting to think. That's what this country needs—more thinkers. There'll be a day when you don't need a man like me.'

She shook her head. 'You don't mean that, Ben.'

'But I do. We're getting ready to defend a property line and while we do some of us might get killed. Why? Kate has more land than she can ever use. There are acres of land to the east of her range that never see a cow. She could lease the land the Texans need. Or Jeff could lease part of his range, but he probably won't. What's the matter with us, anyhow?'

'How many cattle are coming?'

'From what I hear, twenty-five hundred.'

'Suppose it was five thousand? Suppose it was ten thousand. What should we do then—talk?'

'Sure—but we might not get an answer. We might not get one now.' He finished the coffee, stood up, looked critically at Tish and nodded. 'Keep using your head. Maybe we can work out something to save us a lot of trouble.'

*   *   *

They headed toward the river a little later, Ben, Dave, Milo, Carl, Hank and Iron Kate Salter, riding right along with them. Most had little to say. They had slanted to a point across from the Texans' range. There they reined up. There were hardly any cattle in sight on the other side of the river. If the extra cattle had arrived, at least they had not come this far.

'We'll ride up the line,' Kate said.

'No, I want to talk to the Texans,' Ben said.

'A waste of time.' Kate shook her head. 'You're working for me, Ben Carnaby.'

'That's why I want to see the Texans,' Ben

answered. 'Who wants to ride with me?'

'I'll ride along,' Milo said.

'Me, too.' It was Hank who said that.

'I reckon I'll stay with Kate,' Dave said. 'But it wouldn't hurt any to see what the Texans have got to say.'

Kate scowled at him, but she said, 'All right, we'll go see them, let them talk, but that's all. We hold the line at the river.'

They moved on until they were in sight of the Texans' ranch buildings. They moved nearer and suddenly, abruptly, a rifle bullet screamed above them.

Ben reined up, aware that the others had done the same. Carl grabbed for his rifle, pulled it out of its boot. Kate did that too. She was furious. 'Blasting at us! What's the matter with them, anyhow? Are we gonna take that?'

'One shot,' Ben said. 'It was a warning. It could have been lower, hit someone. There could have been more shots.'

'Then let's get out of here.'

'No, I still want to talk to them,' Ben said.

He pulled his rifle from its boot, found an old, white handkerchief in his pocket, shook it out and tied it to the end of the barrel. After that he lifted it and looked at Kate.

She glared at him. 'What's that for?'

'I'm going on in. Want to go with me?'

'Under a white flag? Not me.'

'I'll go along,' Milo said.

'Good. But keep your hand away from your

gun.' Ben motioned to the others. 'Wait here for us.'

Kate spoke up quickly. 'I'll go with you.'

'All right,' Ben agreed. 'You stay here, Milo. Two is enough to ride in.'

Ben led the way, holding the rifle pointed to the sky, the white handkerchief serving as a flag of truce. There was no more shooting and no one in sight as they rode in, but when they reined up two men came out on the porch, another appeared in the barn doorway, and a fourth showed up at the edge of the bunkhouse.

'They're all around us,' Kate muttered.

'Don't worry about it,' Ben said. 'And let me do the talking.' He raised his voice. 'What was the idea of the warning shot?'

'Just that,' said one of the men on the porch. 'We was raided last night and the night before. Didn't know who you were or what you wanted.'

'We did no raiding,' Ben said, and he motioned toward his companion. 'This is Kate Salter. She owns the range across from you. I'm working for her. My name is Carnaby.'

The man on the porch doing the talking touched his hat and said, 'Morning, ma'am. Heard about you. And you too, Carnaby. I'm Eddie Bryan.'

He was a big, thick-bodied man, gray-haired and much older than Chico Kelly. He spoke slowly, heavily. Ben had the sudden feeling

106

that the man was not very well.

'The way we understand it,' Ben said, 'you've got some cattle on the way.'

The man hesitated but then nodded. 'Yes, we do, but I don't know that it's any of your business.'

'Where'll you graze them?' Ben asked bluntly.

'Here, for a few days,' Bryan said. 'Then we'll move some of them to another range, one that we're gonna take over.'

'Where?'

'One that Chico arranged for. Anyhow, that's our problem, Carnaby. It's no concern of yours.'

'I'd still like to know where you're moving them,' Ben said stubbornly.

'Chico ought to be back tomorrow,' Bryan said. 'Or if you got to know sooner, then talk to George Matthews. He's the man Chico is working with.'

'Matthews,' Ben said thoughtfully.

'He's the banker in town, arranged to sell us this range. You ought to know him, Carnaby.'

'I know him,' Ben said. 'One more thing. When do your cattle get here?'

'They ought to make it to the west pastures by tomorrow night—be all around the ranch by the next day.'

Kate spoke under her breath. 'By the third day they'll be to the river. Then what, Ben? They haven't bought any more land. Where would they get it?'

Ben didn't answer. He spoke to Bryan. 'I'd like to see Chico when he gets here. Can I stop by tomorrow?'

'I reckon so. Just don't ride in with an army.'

'I don't have an army,' Ben said. 'And I'm not building one. Be seeing you, Bryan.'

He nodded to Kate, turned away and she followed him. They headed back to join the others. Ben untied his handkerchief from the rifle barrel, put the handkerchief away and returned the rifle to its boot. He spoke half under his breath. 'Matthews!' Then he glanced at Kate. 'How well do you know George Matthews?'

She looked at him, then looked away. 'What do you mean by that?'

'Bryan said that Chico was working with Matthews. What did he mean by that?'

'It doesn't mean anything,' Kate said. 'The Texans are bringing in more cattle and they're using the cattle to spread out, gobble up more land. It ain't gonna work east of the river. If anyone backs off, it'll be Jeff Lorimer.'

'We could join him.'

'Never.'

'Two people can stand up better than one.'

'Not if the two people are me and Jeff Lorimer. Let him fight his own battles. I'll fight mine.'

They reached the others and Ben reported

108

what had been said. If Bryan had been truthful they had three days, counting today, before there would be trouble on the river.

They started back toward their own range.

'Three days,' Kate said grimly. 'We'll be ready for them.'

He made no answer. There were only six of them to defend the line. If the Texas cows moved in at the river and moved on, he and the others might gun down a hundred of them, or even two hundred, but that wouldn't stop the others. And the Texans wouldn't just sit by and watch while their cattle was being slaughtered—they'd be shooting, too, but not at the cattle.

That was what Kate was facing.

It was what Jeff Lorimer was facing.

They were in the same corner but couldn't see it.

After they reached the river they had their noon meal, then, because Kate insisted on it, they rode the river bordering her own range, opposite to the Texans'. She wanted to point out three of the danger points, places where the trees and shrubbery were thin and where the Texas cows might try to break across.

'We can stay under cover,' Kate said. 'There are only six of us, but six can be an army.'

Ben listened to her, studying the terrain. If there was a drive on the river he would be the one to decide what to do about it.

It was late in the afternoon when they got

back to the ranch, and a man was there waiting for them. It was Andy Thorne, and amazingly, he was wearing a deputy's badge. He seemed a little embarrassed about it.

'Didn't want to take the job,' he said gruffly. 'But someone had to do it, and I wasn't doing anything so I thought I might as well try it. I'll do what I can.'

'What happened to Brazos Fowler?' Kate asked.

Andy looked away. 'Don't know, exactly. There was some trouble at the jail. I think Brazos got hurt. His right hand was bandaged but he said he could look after himself, left-handed. Don't know about that. He's left town.'

'And you're taking his place,' Kate said. 'How is Fred Gibbons?'

'I think he's gonna be all right but he won't talk about what happened. He won't be able to go back to work for a couple of weeks.' He turned to Ben. 'Want to talk to you for a minute.'

'Sure. Talk ahead,' Ben said.

Ben left his horse at the corral fence, then walked with Andy to the corner of the barn.

'There's trouble in town,' Andy said. 'I'm supposed to bring you in. If you won't ride in with me tonight, I'm supposed to get a posse.'

'Who says so?'

'Matthews is doing most of the talking. It seems you broke into his house, endangered his wife. He had you jailed, but you broke out.'

'Are you working for Matthews?'

'Nope, for the town. But there's others who are backing up Matthews.'

'Who?'

'Yancy, for one. John Hollis. And a few others.'

'So you're under pressure?'

Andy grunted, nodding. He looked at Ben, then looked away. 'Don't want to make any issue, but if I take a job I like to do it, do what I should.'

'I guess that's the way to feel,' Ben said.

'You gonna ride in with me?'

'No, I'm not.'

Andy moistened his lips. 'My gun is mighty handy. I'm pretty good with it. I could whip it up, cover you. If I had to . . .'

'What?'

'I want you to ride in with me.'

'How long did you work for me?'

'Two years. More'n that.'

'Yes, and we got along fairly well. I like you, Andy, but if you reach for your gun—then go all the way, for that's what I'll do. You'll have to gun me down or I'll do that to you.'

Andy stiffened. His hand was inches from his gun. He was perspiring and breathing faster. For a full minute he didn't speak.

Ben waited.

'You mean it, don't you?' Andy said finally.

'Yes, I mean it.'

'Gusss I'll have to get the posse.'

'Go ahead.'

The man shook his head, relaxing. 'Didn't want to do this anyhow. Didn't want to take the job, but I did. Guess I better head back to town.' He turned away, started toward his horse but stopped, and said, 'Ben, they got you boxed. Only chance you've got is to back out, but I guess you won't do that.'

'No, I won't do that,' Ben said.

'Probably won't need the posse,' Andy said.

VIII

Ben had something more to think about that night. According to Andy he was trapped, didn't have a chance unless he quit taking an interest in what was happening in the basin. But who had trapped him and why? Were the Texans planning to spread out, taking what they wanted by force? Or was the conflict inevitable because of the stubbornness and blindness of nearly everyone involved?

He sat on the porch after supper, watching the shadows gathering. Kate had gone to her room; Tish was busy in the kitchen. Several of the men had gathered in one of the cabins, but now Dave Eckert came outside, noticed Ben on the porch and walked toward him.

'Doing anything important?' he asked.

'Thinking,' Ben answered. 'Or trying to.'

'Been busy that way myself,' Dave said. 'Don't think I'm getting anywhere.' He walked over to the steps, sat down.

'Think there's any chance we could get Kate and Jeff Lorimer together?' Ben asked.

'No chance at all.'

'What would Kate say about leasing some of her land to the Texans?'

'She'd say no. She'd probably yell it. No Texas cow can cross the river.'

'Jeff Lorimer isn't using all his land. Do you

think he might lease some of it?'

'Nope. I don't think he would.'

'Then let's talk about Matthews. What's he most interested in?'

'Money.'

'What does he think about his son?'

'Not much. I could be wrong, but I doubt it.'

'George Matthews sold the Rowland property. That's not a very large place. Do you think that Matthews, in order to make the sale, might have promised the Texans to get them more land?'

'I think Matthews would have said anything to make a sale.'

'Where would he get more land?'

'He didn't have to know. All he wanted to do was make a sale.'

Ben shook his head slowly. 'No, I don't think you're right. If Matthews said he could get more land he must have had something in mind—a part of Kate's land, a part of Lorimer's, or even a part of Red Mesa.'

'Who would want the mesa?'

'With more water it could be used, and I'll bet some of the ranchers on the mesa would be glad to sell some of their land for cash. It's a possibility.'

'A last possibility?'

The door opened suddenly. Kate looked out. She said, 'Dave, can you come in for a moment? I want to talk to you.'

'Sure. Be right there.' Dave stood up,

headed for the door, went inside and closed it.

Ben sat where he was, on the porch. It was growing darker. His thoughts went back to Andy Thorne and he shifted uneasily. Why had Andy hinted that he was trapped? What did he know that Ben didn't know?

The door opened again. This time it was Tish and she said, 'I heard you talking to Dave a few minutes ago. I wanted to see if you were still here. I'll get your money.'

'No. Come here first,' Ben said. 'I want to ask you something. Andy was here when we rode in. Did you talk to him?'

'Some.' She came out on the porch, closed the door. 'It was late when he got here. I had only a few minutes with him. He mentioned one thing that might interest you.'

'What's that?'

'He asked where you were. I said that you and the others were riding the river line, and he said that Jeff Lorimer was much better prepared than you. He said Mr. Lorimer had brought in a dozen hard-looking men, and that more were on the way.'

'A dozen men—and more coming. Where from?'

'I didn't ask him.'

'Did he say anything else?'

'He asked if Hank Matthews was here, and why he had come. I said I didn't know, that I hardly knew him. Why did he come, Ben?'

'To find himself.'

'Is that a riddle?'

'No, I meant what I said.' He scowled, but then nodded. 'Kate said that Hank was no good. That's about the general opinion everywhere. Blame it on him, or on an over-indulgent father. Blame it on his mother's strictness. I don't know who's to blame. Hank told me he wanted to prove something to himself. Maybe he'll find what he wants.'

'Ben, I think—'

The crash of a rifle shot interrupted her. There was another and another. Ben could hear the snapping sound of the bullets smashing into the walls of the house. The shots seemed to be coming from the deep shadows west of the house.

He had jerked to his feet at the sound of the first shot and he lunged at the girl, caught her in one arm, carried her to the floor of the porch. She cried out, maybe because of the not very gentle way he handled her. He landed hard on the floor; she must have hit just as hard and a moment later she was being rolled over the edge of the porch, Ben right with her. It was another three-foot fall to the ground, another hard bump.

Bullets were still smashing into the house and into the cabins. Ben thought someone in one of the cabins was firing back, but he wasn't sure of that. He had fallen half on the girl's body, one leg across hers, his arm across her chest, and he was holding his handgun. He

116

couldn't remember drawing it. He must have grabbed the gun without thinking.

Three more rifle shots smashed into the house. There were more shots fired at the cabins, then, abruptly, the outside firing stopped, although someone in one of the cabins fired several more times, fired out into the darkness.

A sharp silence followed the shooting. Ben couldn't hear the sounds of any horses riding away. Most likely the men firing at the buildings had tied their horses away from the house, had walked in, then at a safe distance had started firing. Right now, the men were walking out, headed back toward their horses.

Tish spoke suddenly. 'Are you going to keep me here forever, or can I get up?'

He shook his head. 'I want you to stay where you are. I think the men who were shooting at us have left, but I don't want you to get up until I'm sure.'

'Do you have to smother me, keep me pinned to the ground?'

He moved the leg across her body, then his arm, aware that it had been pressing down across the soft mounds of her breasts. He spoke slowly. 'I didn't mean to get rough, but there wasn't any time to plan anything. Bullets were hitting everywhere.'

'It was bad enough when you slammed me to the floor,' Tish said. 'Then you pushed me

117

off the porch and fell on top of me. Tomorrow I'll be black and blue everywhere.'

'You're still alive,' Ben said gruffly.

She was silent for a moment, then she surprised him. 'Yes, I am. Thanks, Ben.'

He stared at her, but it was too dark to see her clearly. Her face was a white oval in the shadows. He touched her lightly. 'I didn't mean to hurt you, Tish.'

'I'll be all right. What are a few bruises? Who do you think the men were—the Texans?'

'No, I don't think so. That doesn't make sense. The Texans were raided, too.'

'Jeff Lorimer's men were responsible for that.'

'Would Lorimer have raided us?'

'No. I don't think he would.'

'Then he might not have raided the Texans.'

'But who did? And who was shooting at us?'

'Maybe some outlaws.'

'Outlaws! But why?'

He shook his head, sat up. 'Don't ask me, Tish. Nothing makes sense anymore. Kate, Matthews, Jeff Lorimer and the Texans ought to talk about where we're going, but none of them want to. If I could only—'

He broke off. Kate had come to the door, she was shouting, 'Ben! Ben Carnaby, where are you? What's happened to you?'

'I'm right here,' Ben said, and he stood up. 'I've been dodging bullets.'

'Huh!' She sounded disgusted. Then she snapped out an order. 'Saddle your horse. Get the others and get them saddled. We're riding after them.'

'After who?' Ben asked.

'After the men who blasted us—the Texans.'

'We don't know it was the Texans,' Ben said.

'Who else could it have been?'

'I don't know,' Ben answered. 'But we can see better in the morning. We can shoot better. And if we've got to go after the Texans, they'll still be there. They're not moving out of the basin.'

Dave, who was behind her, spoke up suddenly. 'He's right, Kate. It's a fool thing to ride off in the night. Why don't we wait until morning?'

The woman hesitated, then she said, 'Why do you always have to go against me? Go see if any of the men were hurt. Let me know.'

'Right away,' Dave said.

He left the house and moved past Ben, and headed toward the cabins. Kate stepped back into the house, closing the door behind her.

Ben looked down at Tish. 'You can get up now. If Kate had found you here, I don't know what she'd think.'

'It would be scandalous,' Tish said.

'That's right,' Ben said. He pulled her to her feet and into his arms, and he held her for a moment, then leaned over and kissed her. She had stiffened, but made no struggle.

119

Ben let her go. He said gruffly, 'Take care of yourself. I don't want anything to happen to you.'

She stepped away and said, with a teasing sound in her voice, 'No bruises from anyone but you.'

'No, and I don't mean to bruise,' Ben said. 'Come back here.'

'No, I haven't finished my work in the kitchen,' Tish said, and she hurried up the porch steps.

* * *

Dave Eckert and Carl Hughes rode out the next morning, as soon as it was light. They were to find out what they could learn about the raiders. In less than an hour they were back. By this time the others had finished breakfast and saddled up and Tish was busy putting up lunches.

'There were seven of them,' Dave reported. 'They left their horses back in a clump of trees near the meadow spring, walked in, peppered us with shots, then walked out, reached their horses and rode off.'

'Which way did they come from?' Kate asked.

'Northwest.'

'And when they left?'

'Same direction. Northwest.'

'Straight toward the Texans,' Kate said, and

looked at Ben.

'All right, we'll follow their trail,' Ben said.

'I knew where they were going,' Kate said. 'We could've started earlier, didn't need a trail.'

'We'll still follow it,' Ben said.

They picked up the trail, an easy one to follow. It slanted toward the Rowland range and after they crossed the Cougar River it seemed to point straight toward the Texans' buildings.

No one had much to say. Finally Milo Burke said, 'Something wrong with this. No raiders I ever heard about left a trail as clear as this.'

'Could be they meant to leave a trail,' Ben said.

'Why?'

'They wanted us to follow them.'

They came in sight of the ranch buildings. The trail headed straight toward the buildings. Ben looked that way. A man came out of the ranch house. He might have called out an alarm, for another man came out, then a woman, and a third man appeared from the barn.

Dave Eckert, who had been studying the trail, made a comment. 'The men we been watching must have started galloping their horses about here. You can tell by the stride of the horses and the way they dug into the earth.'

'In a hurry to get home,' Kate said. 'Get

your rifles!'

'No. No rifles,' Ben said. 'The trail we're following will lead straight through the yard ahead. It'll sweep past the Texans' buildings, and keep going.'

Kate reined up. 'What are you trying to tell us?'

'I'm trying to think what this means,' Ben answered. 'Just like Milo said, no raiders ever left a trail easy to follow, unless there was a reason. The men who hit us last night wanted us to follow the trail—straight here. They wanted us to blame the Texans. Instead, why don't we ask them if some men went tearing through here about dawn. Seven men, riding hard.'

'Sure, that's what they'll say,' Kate answered. 'And they'll be lying.'

But she scowled as she said that, and she hesitated.

Straight ahead, the three men and the woman were waiting in the yard. One of the men was Eddie Bryan; the woman was Mrs. Kelly.

Ben raised both hands as he rode in, the others followed him. He called out, 'Hello, there. I don't suppose Chico Kelly is back.'

'He's back,' Bryan said. 'But he had to head for town. Expect him back toward dusk.'

Ben nodded. 'Want to tell me what happened this morning, along toward sunup.'

'Nothing,' the man answered. 'But about

two hours earlier, at about three o'clock, a crowd of men rode through the yard. They came at full gallop, yelling and firing their rifles. Only one of them stopped, and he didn't mean to. He got in the way of a bullet.'

'Was he badly hurt?'

'Killed. His body's in the barn. Chico will make a report to the sheriff.'

'Where did the men go after they rode through here?' Ben asked.

'They swung north, into the Ute Hills,' Bryan said. 'They've hit us twice before. That's where their trail led, almost due north. If we weren't waiting for our cattle we would've gone after them.'

'Can I see the man you killed?'

'Suit yourself,' Bryan said, and he motioned toward the barn.

Ben dismounted, trailed the reins of his horse.

'I want to see him, too,' Kate said, and swung to the ground.

The others dismounted, joining them. Everyone trooped into the barn excepting Mrs. Kelly, who waited at the door.

The man who had been killed had been covered by a blanket. One of the Texans' riders stripped the blanket away, then stepped aside. Ben looked down at the man but was unable to recognize him. Kate shook her head. Most were silent, but Hank Matthews made a comment. 'I've seen him in town. I'm almost sure of that. He was with Brazos Fowler.'

Ben looked at Bryan. 'Did he carry any papers, any identification? Have you any notion who he was?'

'None at all,' Bryan said.

Ben turned away, moved out into the yard. The others followed him. He stared to the north.

'So that's where the men headed,' he said slowly. 'Into the Ute Hills—my hills, or at least that's where my ranch was. Wonder if the same men burned me out . . . they probably did. They could have.'

'Hey, look! There they come!' Bryan said, and he sounded excited. He pointed to the west.

Ben, and everyone else, turned and looked to the west. There was movement on the western horizon, a spreading, rolling movement. These were the first of the new cattle plodding across the land. A thin pall of dust hung above them. There was a point rider to the north and another to the south, heading the herd, keeping the leaders in line. Most of the other riders weren't in sight.

'Twenty-five hundred in that herd,' Bryan said. 'Could be there's almost three thousand. Ever see a sight like that?'

'Where you going to keep them?' Ben asked.

'Chico's arranging for that now.'

'You won't push them on my land,'

Kate said.

Bryan didn't seem to hear her. He was watching the approaching cattle, nodding in approval. He seemed wholly unworried about where they would be grazed.

Kate spoke again. 'Look here, Bryan. Post some riders on the river. If any of those cows cross over onto my land, there's gonna be trouble.'

'Sure, sure,' Bryan said. 'We'll keep them close herded until we get the pasture we need.' He pointed again to the west. 'Ain't that a sight to see, rolling across the land?'

Kate shook her head. She turned to Ben. 'Let's get out of here, get back to the river. We'll make our stand tomorrow.'

IX

They turned south after they left the Texans' ranch. Ben insisted on that. He wanted to see if Jeff Lorimer had put up guards along the edge of his range—and it seemed he had. They headed east again when they came to the fence bordering this range and Lorimer's and they passed three men who seemed to be watching it. There could have been more men to the west, where the danger was greater.

Tish had told Ben that Lorimer had brought in a dozen men and that more were coming. Even if he had twenty or thirty, Ben doubted that Lorimer could keep the cattle from sweeping onto his land if they turned in that direction. A fence—and men—could go down under the pressure of a surging drive.

When they reached the road up the basin, and the river, Kate said bluntly, 'Dave, you head for the house. I've got a supply wagon ready, loaded with grub and extra blankets. Hitch a team to it and start it this way. Tish can drive it. If she don't want to, she can go home.'

'Are we going to camp on the river?' Ben asked.

'Yep. That's it,' Kate said. 'We're gonna hold the line, hell to breakfast. Any argument about that?'

126

He shrugged, making no comment. Kate could be as hard as any man, and just as profane. Ben could admire some of her traits, but not all of them—not her blindness, her antagonism to Jeff Lorimer, or her readiness to hold the line at the river. She should have talked to Lorimer, Matthews and the Texans. To defend the river line should have been a last step, not the first.

*   *   *

They rode the river line from the southeast corner of the Texans' range to the northeast corner, close to the bluffs edging Red Mesa. Ben doubted they would have much trouble at either end of the line. If the Texans tried to move their cattle over the river they would most likely make the attempt at one of the three places where lumbering operations had thinned out the trees. And he doubted that anything would happen right away. If an attempt was made to cross the river it would be planned; it would be a concerted drive using not only cattle but men.

Kate had already picked out a campsite, near one of the danger points, but under some nearby trees. When they rode in along toward dusk, a fire had already been started and Tish was standing near it, keeping an eye on the cooking supper. A brisk wind had loosened her hair and had added color to her cheeks. Ben

127

had wanted her to come, but now he wished she hadn't. This could be a danger point in a day or two.

They had supper, then picked places to settle down for the night. 'The men are to bunk north of the wagon,' Kate decided. 'The women are to bunk to the south—you men, keep on your side of the line.'

'Lines!' Milo said. 'That's all we hear about.'

'It's what we live by,' Kate said. 'Anyone want to back out?'

'Not yet,' Milo said, and grinned. 'Nothing's happened.'

'It will,' Kate snapped.

Ben stared into the fire. It seemed to him that Kate was enjoying this, having the time of her life. Here, suddenly, was a touch of adventure, a promise of violence. They had been raided last night and at the Texans' ranch a man had been killed. More conflict was ahead, but Kate didn't seem to mind at all. From the way she was acting, she loved it. He had never seen this facet of her character. It was something new, different—and frightening.

It had turned dark but the fire was still burning high, sending out a lot of light. He could see Tish working at the supply wagon, a dozen steps away. It was nice to have a fire like this, but tomorrow he was going to rule against it.

128

Dave walked over to the fire, leaned over to pick up the coffeepot. 'Anyone want seconds?' he asked.

As he straightened up, about to pour out a cupful, a rifle shot exploded somewhere in the darkness. The bullet hit him in the right shoulder, twisting him around. He staggered back. There was another rifle shot, and another. Dave cried out, lost his balance, and plunged to the ground, still absurdly holding the coffeepot and cup.

There was more shooting from the darkness. Carl Hughes came to his feet, gave a hoarse cry and got down again. He must have been hit, for he rolled over his side.

Ben threw himself back on the ground. He yelled at Tish, shouted her name. 'Tish! Down on the ground!'

He kept rolling away, aware of the confusion around the fire. The outlaws, who had raided them last night, had moved in toward their campsite as soon as it was safely dark. They had moved in close, and when they were ready they had started firing with no warning. It was a deadly ambush, vicious and merciless, ruthless.

Dave Eckert and Carl Hughes had been hit and another man cried out—Ben thought it was Hank Matthews.

Suddenly Kate screamed. He was sure it was Kate, not Tish. He had seen Kate get up and start running, but then she went down. She might have tripped, or she might have been hit by a bullet.

Tish! What about her? He looked toward the wagon twice, but didn't see her. Maybe she had dropped to the ground and stayed there, or she might have been hurt.

Ben rolled out of the circle of light. He wasn't safe and he knew it. He ought to keep on rolling, keep low and move away—that ought to be what he was doing. Instead, he stopped. Someone noticed him rolling away, fired at him twice. He edged past some shrubbing plant, still flat to the ground. He hadn't been hit—yet—and he clutched his handgun.

A huge, bulking figure moved out of the darkness, started toward the fire—a man trailing a rifle. Ben used his handgun, dropped him.

He saw another dim figure and fired again, and the man went down and started screaming. That took care of two of the enemy—whoever they were. Now, if another man would show up . . .

Two other men did. One was behind the fire. The other was nearer the light. Ben fired at the man who was farther away, dropped him. He swung his gun toward the other, but he was on his knees by then, and might be visible. A bullet tugged at the shoulder of his coat, another seemed to tear into the side of his head. He felt a sudden, sharp pain and

130

went blind, but he fired his gun and hoped his aim was good.

Pain smashed him again, and for a time, then, he remembered nothing.

Someone was telling him something, but the voice seemed far, far away. He tried to listen, but he blacked out. The voice spoke again. This time it seemed to be coming from straight above him, a woman's voice; it was Tish, and she sounded provoked. 'I wish you would lie still and quit hitting at me. I'm trying to help you.'

He opened his eyes. It was still dark but he could see; his eyes were all right. His head hurt terribly, there was a stabbing pain in his arm, and his stomach was churning. He remembered the sudden, devastating attack. It was amazing he was alive.

He said, 'Tish?'

'Yes, Ben.' She was right beside him.

'The others . . .'

'Milo wasn't hurt. He helped me get you on a horse. We rode down the river about two miles, stopped here. Milo went somewhere. He said he'd be back as soon as he could.'

Ben thought about that for a moment, then started to ask about Kate, but even while he was talking he fell asleep.

*   *   *

It was light when he woke up and it seemed he

was alone in a small clearing in the trees. He looked to either side but could see no one else, no horse, no sign that anyone was near. His head still throbbed, the wound in his arm still hurt. After a time he sat up, but that made him dizzy and he lay down again.

The brushing sound of footsteps startled him. He reached instinctively for his gun, but his holster was empty. He didn't need it anyhow. It was Tish who was walking toward him, tall, thin, a frown on her face.

Her frown disappeared when she saw he was awake and she cried, 'Ben, I've been worried. You've slept all morning.'

'I probably needed it,' Ben said. 'How bad is this bullet gash on my head?'

'It scraped the bone. It bled quite a bit, but the bleeding has stopped.'

'And my arm?'

'The bullet went through the fleshy part of your upper arm. It's swollen and I know it hurts, but if there's no infection . . .'

'Has Milo come back?'

'Not yet.'

'I meant to ask about Kate.'

She shook her head. 'We don't know about her. I heard her scream right after the shooting started but later I couldn't find her. Milo couldn't either. She might have—wandered into the trees.'

'And the others?'

She looked away, and when she spoke her

voice was low, strained. 'They're dead—all three—Dave Eckert, Carl Hughes and Hank Matthews. I—I don't want to talk about them.'

'All right, we won't,' Ben said, and was silent, but questions were pounding through his head. Why hadn't Milo and Tish been able to find Kate? Or if she had escaped, how had she managed it? And the outlaws had been hired by someone, they had been part of a plan, a very well-conceived plan. But who was behind it?

'Wouldn't you like a drink?' Tish asked suddenly.

He nodded, still thinking.

'And something to eat?'

'Yes, if you brought anything.'

'Milo remembered to,' Tish said. 'I'll get some water, then we'll see about food.'

He smiled, closed his eyes again. He was glad Milo had escaped the attack. Milo must have hit the ground at the sound of the first shot, then started rolling away. Now that the real trouble had begun, he could be miles from here, and should keep riding, but maybe he was still around. Ben hoped he was.

Ben had a drink, some warm soup and some meat and bread. Then he slept for a time, and after he woke up, with the girl's help, he got to his feet and tried walking. He was a little dizzy, a little shaky, but he managed all right. He sat down again and rested.

Milo had not yet returned, and no one else

had bothered them.

It was late afternoon by this time. Ben found his gun near where he had been lying. He reloaded it, slid it into his holster. Tish frowned, shuddered when he checked it, but she made no comment.

They had supper as it was growing dark.

Milo still had not returned. Tish said she was worried about him. 'But you're not going after him,' she said definitely. 'You're going to stay here.'

'I wouldn't know where to look for him,' Ben said. 'He'll make it back here, or he won't. We'll wait until morning.'

'Then what?'

'I don't know, Tish; we'll work out something.'

'We could ride to Red Mesa.'

'What would we do there?'

'Wait, I suppose, until we knew how things were.'

'What if Kate was still somewhere around?'

'Is there a chance she is?'

'I think there's a chance. Even some of the worst men wouldn't want to shoot a woman. Besides, if the rest of us were finished, Kate would seem helpless. Yes, she might be still around.'

'And you think you owe her something?'

'Three months of work,' Ben said. 'And, besides, I'm interested in what happens here in the basin. Near as I know, that hasn't been decided.'

'But with no one riding the river . . .'

Ben shook his head. 'The law is still the law; property rights are fixed. The Texans can't use Kate's range unless they buy the land or lease it, legally. Squatters' rights no longer stand up in court.'

She was silent for a moment, then she said, 'You mean that what happened last night isn't—isn't the end of the trouble?'

'No. Not the end.'

'I sort of wish it was, Ben. When I think about last night . . .'

'Don't think about it. Think about tomorrow.'

'Tomorrow, and more trouble like last night.'

'A different trouble, maybe not so serious.'

'It won't be,' Tish said. 'That's why I'd like to head for Red Mesa.'

'Or the Ute Hills.'

'If the outlaws weren't there.'

'We'll get rid of them,' Ben said.

* * *

The next morning Ben awoke to the sound of a horse splashing along the river.

He turned toward the girl, and spoke in a low voice. 'Tish! Wake up. There's someone over near the river.'

She sat up, stiffened, caught her breath.

135

'Don't make a sound,' he whispered. 'Stay where you are. Don't say a word.'

He reached for his gun, found it, half sat up and waited.

The sounds of footsteps reached him. He was hoping it was Milo, but he couldn't be sure of it.

A voice spoke from across the clearing. 'Ben! Tish! It's me—Milo.'

Ben relaxed. He could sense the relief Tish must have felt, and he called out, 'Yep, we're here. Move right in.'

Tish got quickly to her feet. 'Milo, we worried about you.'

'No need to be,' Milo answered. 'Although I wouldn't say this was the most friendly place in the world. How do you feel, Ben?'

'I'll be able to ride,' Ben said.

'You shouldn't,' Tish said. 'You ought to rest for at least another day.'

'Next time,' Ben said. 'What can you tell me about the raid?'

'I'll tell you what I can,' Milo said. 'Some things I have to guess about. When the shooting started I hit the ground, and started rolling, crawling. When I got away from the fire I looked back. It was nearly over by then. Three men were down. Kate was yelling and heading away from the fire. I didn't see Tish anywhere. Or you. I didn't know what had happened to you.'

'I rolled away, too,' Ben said.

136

'I know; I found out when the outlaws started in toward the fire to make sure everyone was dead. You opened up with your gun, got two of them. You wounded another. That was enough for them. I heard one yell to another that they could come back when it was light, and when it was safe. Then they walked out. I found Tish, then I found you. You were trying to get up. We looked for Kate but couldn't find her. One of our horses was gone. I think she got away.'

Ben was frowning. 'Do you think they let her go?'

'I think there were only five or six men— maybe seven. They were pretty busy. Could be they just didn't shoot at Kate or each man shot somewhere else until it was too late.'

'Where have you been?'

'Back to where they hit us. They said they'd come back but they didn't. I even waited most of the night.'

'What a damned fool thing to do. You could have been killed.'

'I wasn't. I was a damned fool when I rolled away and found I'd lost my gun. Next time, I'll grab my gun first.'

Ben knew this was hard on Tish, but he had to ask, 'What about the men who were killed? Did you do anything about them?'

'I haven't yet.'

'Someone's got to.'

'All right, we'll ride back soon as we eat.

137

How about it, Tish?'

'It won't be like a breakfast,' Tish said.

'Anything will do,' Milo said.

Ben looked up at the sky. The shadows were not as deep as they had been. It might turn out to be a warm, clear day. He hoped so. They were not starting out very well—with a cold breakfast, a ride in the cool of the morning—then a burial.

He peered in the direction of Milo Burke. 'You still riding with me?'

'Yep, I guess I will. There's only two of us. Think we can do anything?'

'We'll find out,' Ben said quietly.

X

They rode back upriver to the camp, where they had been ambushed. Tish reined up short, stayed in the saddle. She was to stand guard. Ben and Milo moved in closer, dismounted, tied their horses, and for the next hour were busy.

They rejoined Tish after they had done what had to be done. Ben was already tired. What had happened this morning had been a sobering experience. Death was a brutal fact.

'Which way?' Milo asked.

'Over to the road, then north. We'll ride as far as the foot of the mesa.' He looked at Tish. 'You're going home.'

'I was afraid of that,' Tish said. 'I don't want to go. If there's any way . . .'

'There isn't.'

'Then if I've got to go home I know the way. You don't have to go with me.'

'We've got all day.'

She shook her head. 'You've been wounded. You shouldn't ride anywhere. Every mile hurts. There's really no reason you have to ride with me to the mesa.'

Milo agreed with her. 'You shouldn't be riding any more'n you've got to. Tish won't have any trouble getting home.'

Ben hesitated, but he finally agreed. He

said, 'Straight home, Tish.'

'Don't worry about me, please.'

'I won't. I'll be up there to see you in a day or two.'

'You'd better,' Tish said, and her lips twitched. Then she raised her hand, waved. 'Take care of yourself, Ben. You too, Milo. Be seeing you.'

She wheeled away, headed for the road. When she reached it she headed north in the direction of the mesa.

'She'll do all right,' Milo said. 'She did pretty well, night before last. Some women would have gone to pieces.'

Ben nodded, then he took a look at Milo. 'Want to start taking chances?'

'If it'll lead toward the men who ambushed us.'

'We ought to get there soon enough. I want to start with the Texans.'

'Fair enough,' Milo said, and he grinned. 'They ought to be getting used to us, we've been there enough.'

They headed west to the road and as they crossed it Ben looked to the north. Tish had disappeared over a curve of the land. In another hour she ought to be climbing to the mesa, out of any immediate danger.

Within two miles they came to the first Texas cows and there were quite a few of them. Then, almost at once, they saw two riders headed toward them. They'd probably been riding the herd, trying to keep them from spreading toward the river. Both were armed, but they didn't seem antagonistic.

'Anything we can do for you?' one asked.

'We're on our way to see Chico Kelly,' Ben answered.

'Might be home,' the man answered. 'Or he might be out riding. Eddie Bryan will probably be there.'

'Then we'll talk to him,' Ben said. 'Any reason we shouldn't?'

'Nope.' The man grinned. 'Just hope you can make it through the cattle. There's quite a few between here and the house.'

'We'll try to push through,' Ben said.

He and Milo moved on. There seemed to be cattle everywhere. They had no trouble riding through them, but from the number of them, Ben could tell that in another day or so the cattle would have to move on. They would be out of grass.

'Three to four thousand cattle!' Ben muttered. 'The Texans need three times as much range as they've got. What are they going to do next week?'

'Move them on,' Milo said.

They came in sight of the ranch building, pulled into the yard and reined up. Eddie Bryan came out on the porch.

He waved a hand. 'You must have come through some of our new cattle. How did they look?'

'Lean and hungry,' Ben answered. 'Where you gonna graze them?'

'South of here.'

'It's Lorimer's range, south of here.'

'Used to be. Nope, I guess that's not true. We don't get possession for five more days.'

'You mean Jeff Lorimer is selling out?'

'Nope. Not quite. He's selling us half of his range. I wish we could get more but this was the best deal we could make.'

Ben shook his head. It was hard to believe that Bryan was telling the truth. From what Lorimer had told him the man wouldn't sell an acre. He had declared he would hold the line at his north boundary. He had even brought in a crew of hardcase riders. What had happened to them? What had made Lorimer change his mind?

'Let me ask you something,' he said slowly. 'You told me you'd been bothered by raiders. How about last night, or the night before?'

'Haven't seen anything of them,' Bryan said. 'And if I never see them again, that's too soon. What happened to you?'

Ben touched his bandaged head. 'A near miss. Not important.'

That wasn't quite true. The wound at the side of his head still throbbed. His arm hurt even worse. He was lucky in one respect—the bullet wound was in his left arm. He would be able to use his gun if he had to.

Three men rode in, then, from the south,

Chico Kelly among them. He waved a greeting to Ben, nodded to Milo, and pulled up in front of the porch.

'Sorry I missed you the other day,' Chico said. 'We've been busy around here. We're still busy. What can I do for you?'

'I'm not sure,' Ben said slowly. 'Bryan tells me you're buying half of Lorimer's range.'

'A little more than half,' Chico said. 'Our south boundary, in five more days, will be along Deer Trail Creek.'

'Why do you have to wait five days?'

'I don't know,' Chico said. 'It has something to do with the matter of the title. Matthews wasn't very clear about it—but at least he was definite about the sale.'

'George Matthews?'

'Yes. He's the one who arranged it.'

'Did you talk to Lorimer?'

'Nope. Worked out the deal with Matthews. He said to leave Lorimer alone, said he was touchy, and that he could work things out better if he was left alone. What's on your mind, Ben?'

'Lorimer.'

'What about him?'

'I used to work with him, know him pretty well.'

'What if you do?'

'I can't believe he would sell half of his range.'

'He must have changed his mind.'

'Or Matthews might have lied.'

'What does that mean?'

'Just what I said.' Ben spoke slowly. 'Suppose, five days from today, Matthews tells you that the deal fell through—that you can't get the land you expected.'

'If anything like that happens,' Chico said bluntly, 'the town will need a new banker—and I mean it.'

'That won't save your cattle.'

Chico shook his head. 'No, I don't have to worry about that. To me, a deal is a deal. It's not something you can rub out. You live up to it. Matthews is going to live up to what he promised, and that's all there is to it. It's my problem, anyhow—not yours.'

'Five days,' Ben said, frowning.

'Five days,' Chico said. 'And that's too long to wait, but we can stand it. We're close herding our cattle.'

'What about your south border? Are there some men guarding it?'

'There were some men there yesterday, now they're gone. I think Lorimer's called them off. They weren't needed anyhow.'

Ben was silent for a moment, then he shook his head. 'This doesn't figure.'

'What doesn't?' Chico was scowling.

'Lorimer wouldn't have sold half his range.'

'He could have changed his mind.'

'Not Lorimer. Did you say you never talked to him?'

'I never talked to him about buying his land. I spoke to him in town once or twice.'

'And you said Matthews told you not to talk to him?'

'That's what he said. I left the matter up to him. What was wrong with that? I made my deal with him—George Matthews.'

'Mind if I talk to Lorimer?'

Chico shook his head, but he stiffened, seemed angry. 'You can do whatever you want to, Ben, but if you ask Lorimer about selling his land, you're butting into my business, and that's something I don't like.'

'It'll be my business if your deal falls through and you decide to push some of your cattle across the river onto Kate Salter's land.'

'I won't be moving that way. I'll be moving my cattle south.'

'And if the deal falls through?'

'Then I'll take the land I need.'

'No, you won't, Chico.'

'You think I won't?' The man paused, then made a sound in his throat. It might have been a laugh, although there was nothing amusing about it. He touched his gun lightly. 'You don't know me, Ben. I can get along just fine, but if I have to I can fight like hell. And I mean it. Don't make any mistakes about me.'

'I'll remember that,' Ben said flatly.

'So what are you going to do?'

'See Lorimer. Then I plan to see Matthews.'

'Stirring up trouble?'

145

'No,' Ben said. 'I'll be trying to unmuddy the water. I want to see what's coming.'

'Then go ahead,' Chico said. 'Hell with you!'

Ben motioned to Milo. 'Let's move out, south.'

*   *   *

In half a mile Ben slowed down. Milo caught up with him, then he looked back, grunting. Ben glanced at him.

'They're watching us,' Milo said. 'I wouldn't even be surprised if they follow us.'

'I half wish they would,' Ben said. He took another look at Milo. 'Suppose you had a small ranch in the basin? Would you bring in twenty-five hundred cattle before you knew where they could be grazed?'

'Nope, I don't think I would.'

'Suppose some man told you he could get you more land?'

'I would want to be damned sure he was right.'

'Would that be enough?'

'I doubt it. I would want an agreement, signed and delivered. I'd want to be sure.'

'Then how about Chico?'

'I'd think he would want to be sure—but then, that's the way I feel. Chico could be different.'

'No, I think he knew, Milo. But I don't know what he knew. Let's see if we can find

146

Lorimer.'

They rode on, headed south, came to the wire fence separating the Texans' land from Lorimer's, and followed it. In about half a mile they came to a place where a post had been snapped and the wire was broken. At that point they crossed into Lorimer's range. Ben looked back several times, but no one seemed to be trailing them.

'I don't mind seeing Lorimer, or even Matthews,' Milo said suddenly. 'Just don't forget those men who ambushed us.'

'They're on the list,' Ben said. 'And they're in this mix-up, too, but I don't know where they belong. They hit the Texans, they hit us. It could be they hit Lorimer. Who are they working for?'

Milo shook his head. 'I don't know who they're working for and I don't care. I just want a chance at them.' He was silent for a moment, looked away, then added, 'Ben, I don't usually get excited about things, never lose my temper, but there's something about that ambush that gets me stirred up—it was so damned sudden. Think about the three men we lost—not a one of them had a chance. It was straight-out murder.'

'Yes, you're right about that,' Ben said.

Milo said, 'You can set the course, but somewhere along the line, find me the men who ambushed us.'

'They might find us first.'

'That would be all right, too,' Milo said.

They rode on, finally coming in sight of the Lorimer ranch buildings. There were no signs of any activity around it—no one in the yard, no saddled horses tied to the corral fence. They rode in closer, pulled into the yard and stopped. Ben called out. 'Lorimer! Come on out. I'd like to talk to you.'

There was no answer.

He called several times but there was no reply.

'There's no one here,' Milo said, shaking his head. 'In a place as big as this, someone ought to be home.'

Ben looked around the kitchen, the barn, the bunkhouse and the cook's cabin but it seemed that everyone was away.

'We'll head for town,' he said finally. 'Lorimer might be there. Or if we miss him we can try Matthews.'

'Isn't he the man who put you in jail?'

'He's the one.'

'And what about Andy Thorne, who's acting sheriff?'

'We'll try to keep out of sight.'

'That might not work out,' Milo said. 'But I suppose we can see what happens.'

*   *   *

They headed for the Cougar River, staying in the bordering trees most of the way toward town, and when they got to Chaparral Creek they turned off and followed it. That took them to the Mexican settlement north of town, where there was a cantina. It was mostly a drinking place, but it also put out Mexican food. They stopped there for their evening meal, so they wouldn't have to risk a meal in town where they might have been noticed.

It was dark when they left the cantina and they met no one on the short ride to town. Ben led the way to the livery stable. Rod Ackerman, who ran the place and who had offered Ben a place to hide, wasn't there. He never locked the barn when he was away, so Ben and Milo left their horses in there. Ben wasn't riding the horse Ackerman had loaned him, but when the man returned he'd recognize Ben's and Milo's horses as belonging to Iron Kate. The stableman might guess that Ben was in town.

That was nothing to worry about. Ackerman was not the man to talk. Ben mentioned that to Milo, then said, 'How about trying the banker, George Matthews?'

'That's all right with me,' Milo said, and he grinned. 'Never had any dealings with a banker. This might be interesting.'

'We'll try his house,' Ben said.

They headed for the banker's house in a roundabout way, and got there without any trouble. There were lights around the shaded windows, an indication that someone was home. Ben and Milo stepped up on the porch and Ben knocked on the door. He waited for a moment, then knocked again.

Matthews came to the door, opened it, and looking into the shadowed porch, asked, 'Who's there?'

'It's me,' Ben said.

He reached out, pushed the door wider, stepped into the hallway again, and found it interesting to watch the way the banker reacted. He backed away, catching his breath, lifted his hands shoulder-high. The skin of his face showed hardly any color, his eyes widened, and he looked terrified.

He cried out, 'No! No! No!'

Ben shook his head. 'Sorry, Matthews. I didn't want to frighten you. I just want to talk to you.' He edged to the side, then spoke to Milo. 'Keep an eye on him. I want to see who's in the parlor.'

The curtained entrance to the parlor was only a step away. He moved in that direction, swept the curtains to the side, but even as he did that, a bullet shot from the parlor screamed past him.

He plunged to the floor, grabbing at his gun. Halfway across the parlor, standing at a table, was a man he had never seen before. He caught a quick look at him, a tall man, thin, stooped, with gun in hand.

The man fired again as Ben hit the floor.

The first bullet hit slightly to the side; the

150

second was too high. There might have been a third shot from the man but he didn't manage it. Ben took the third shot himself. His bullet hit the man squarely in the chest, drove him backward. He fell against a chair, crushed into it.

Mrs. Matthews screamed. She'd been sitting in a rocking chair on the other side of the room, knitting, but she'd dropped her work, and she was staring fixedly at the man who'd been shot.

She screamed again, not so loudly as before, and suddenly clutched her throat with both hands, then crumpled to the floor in a faint. One of her legs stretched out from under her dress. It was thin, black stockinged, but there was a fancy pink garter above her knee. If she had known about that she would have been terribly embarrassed.

'Is everything all right?' Milo called from the hallway.

'No damage,' Ben said, standing up. 'At least, no damage to me.' He turned and looked toward Matthews, who was actually shaking. 'Your wife hasn't been hurt. She fainted, that's all. Who was the man who tried to gun me down?'

The banker moistened his lips. 'I—I—you get out of here.'

'I want to talk to you about Lorimer.'

'You've got nothing to do with him.'

'Is he going to sell his ranch?'

151

'Part of it.'

Ben shook his head. 'I don't believe it.'

'I don't care what you believe,' Matthews cried. 'You've just killed another man. You'll hang for this, Ben Carnaby. You'll hang for it.'

Milo broke in. 'Those shots could have been heard. Want me to look outside?'

'Go through the kitchen,' Ben said. He pointed to the door at the end of the hallway. 'See if the way is clear to get away.'

'Coming with me?'

'Right away.' Ben turned back to the banker. 'Who's the man in the parlor—the one who tried to kill me?'

'His name was Wells. He was a new settler to the basin. You'll pay for this, Carnaby.'

Ben nodded slowly. He was fairly sure that after he left here Matthews would explain that what had happened was the fault of Ben Carnaby. This visit hadn't helped him a bit. What had he learned? Nothing. He still couldn't believe that Lorimer had sold a part of his range.

He said, 'Matthews, where can I find Lorimer?'

'He was here but I think he's gone back to the ranch.'

'He hired some men. What happened to them?'

'He didn't need them after he decided to sell. He must have let them go.'

That sounded reasonable. And it was

152

reasonable that a man might change his mind. Lorimer could have decided he could get along with less land, or he might have needed more money. Ben wondered if he was looking at everything wrong. Was he fighting an enemy who didn't exist?

'Carnaby, you're finished,' Matthews said, and he pointed a shaky finger. 'That man you killed didn't even have a gun.'

'What did you say?' Ben gasped.

'I was here.' Matthews was getting bolder. 'I know what happened. I tell you . . .'

There were voices outside. A crowd was gathering. Ben knew it was time to move out, but he hesitated for another moment. Matthews had just made a ridiculous charge— that the man who had fired at him twice hadn't been armed; but Matthews' lie put him in the right perspective—if he could lie as easily as this, he could lie about anything. Ben had been at the point of believing what Matthews had said about Lorimer. Now, he didn't.

Someone hammered on the front door and a voice outside called, 'Matthews! Matthews, are you all right? What was the shooting?'

Ben headed toward the kitchen but as he passed the banker he said, 'Go ahead, Matthews. Make up another story, but be a little careful. One of these days you'll bump up against the truth—and that's gonna hurt.'

He kept on toward the back door.

XI

It was quiet in Ackerman's barn. Milo was standing at the edge of the doorway, watching the saddling yard and what he could see of the street. Ben was on the other side of the doorway, listening to Rod Ackerman. The stableman had several bits of news. Some of it was quite interesting.

'I knew that Lorimer brought in some men and I know they left,' Ackerman said. 'From what I heard they wanted more money. Lorimer wouldn't pay it, so they quit.'

'And what about selling half of his range?' Ben asked.

'There hasn't even been a whisper like that.' The man shook his head. 'Lorimer ain't the kind to cut down on his range.'

'Has Kate been in town?'

'Haven't seen her.'

'How about Andy? What's he been doing?'

'Strutting. Polishing his badge. He's sure proud of himself. He won't want to give up his job when Gibbons gets well.'

'So Gibbons is getting better. Who slammed him on the head so the outlaws could escape?'

'I went to see him. He said Brazos Fowler was the man, but he's not here anymore. I guess he's pulled out.'

'And the outlaws?' Ben asked. 'Or put it this

154

way—are there many strangers in town?'

'A few. Or maybe there's too many. I've seen better'n a dozen the last few days. A good many of them keep their horses here, but as likely as not, they ride out after dark.'

'Are any out riding tonight?'

'Five of them pulled out just after dark. Don't have any idea where they went. They might have—'

Milo interrupted. 'Someone's coming.'

Ben got quickly to his feet. He kept his voice low. 'Over here, Milo.' Then he turned to the stableman. 'We'll keep out of sight. We're not here, no matter who it is.'

He moved away from the door and around the corner of a stack of baled hay. Milo was with him.

Ackerman waited in the barn doorway. There was enough light outside so that Ben could see him dimly. After a moment the man said, 'Howdy there, Andy. How's everything?'

'Not too good.' Andy's voice was barely audible. 'Seen anything of Ben Carnaby?'

'Nope.' The lie was instant. 'Haven't seen him for days.'

'Like him, don't you?'

'Yep. We got along.'

Andy reached the doorway. His voice was louder. 'If he got in trouble, you'd probably help him.'

'Sure would if I could,' Ackerman said.

'You could even be hiding him now.'

155

'Why? Has he done something wrong?'

'He busted into Matthews' home, gunned a man down—a man who wasn't even armed.'

The stableman shook his head. 'That don't sound like Ben.'

'It sure don't,' Andy said. 'I don't believe the story myself. Wish I could find Ben. I'd like to get his story. If you could help me . . .'

'Wish I could, Andy.'

'It could be he left town,' Andy said. 'I'll be wanting my horse in about an hour.'

'Sure. In about an hour,' Ackerman said.

Andy left, and after he had gone Ben and Milo rejoined the stableman near the barn doorway.

'Seems to me you could have told him you were here,' Ackerman said, frowning. 'Hell, the man worked for you. He even said he didn't believe you shot an unarmed man.'

'He's wearing a badge,' Ben answered. 'When you wear a badge you live up to it.' Ben was silent for a moment, then he said, 'Milo and me have got an errand to run. Want to get our horses ready? We ought to be back in half an hour.'

'If you want a bottle, I've got one.'

Ben laughed, but shook his head. 'We don't need a bottle, but thanks. Come on, Milo.'

They left the barn, crossed the saddling yard and then the street, and kept walking, circling now behind some of the buildings fronting the plaza.

'Where we going?' Milo asked.

'To Laura Digby's,' Ben answered. 'And we're after information—that's all.'

'Strictly business, huh?' The man grinned. 'This'll be a new experience.'

'Do you know any of Laura's girls?'

'One, but I don't know her very well.'

'Mind talking to her? While I was working as sheriff I learned one thing about Laura's girls—they knew more about what was happening in the basin than I could ever know. When a man spends an hour with one of Laura's girls, among other things he usually talks. He might not even realize it.'

Milo said, 'That's something to remember.'

Laura's doorway was shadowed, and even inside, in the parlor, the lights were not very bright. Milo asked for Irma, then waited for her to appear. Ben said he wanted to see Laura, herself. The big wide-shouldered bouncer who admitted them recognized Ben. He was a Mexican, José Porfino, and he said, grinning, 'The sheriff was here looking for you. I hope he will not be back.'

'Tell him I'm still not here,' Ben said.

Laura didn't seem pleased to see Ben. She shook her head, frowning. 'I try never to have trouble here in the house. You ought to know that, Ben.'

'I know it, Laura.'

'Andy Thorne was here, with his big bright badge. He thought you might be here.'

'All right, I'll leave as soon as I can,' Ben said. 'But I want to know a few things. Some new cattle have been brought into the basin—where are they going to be grazed?'

The woman shook her head. 'I don't know. All I can tell you is this—the two Texans who own the cattle are going to get the range they need. It's been promised to them.'

'By Matthews?'

'I didn't say that. You did. And now I'm going to say something. Ben, get your horse and start riding. Start riding and don't stop. If you stay another day that's too long.'

'Who's after me?'

'I'll mention one person but that won't surprise you—Brazos Fowler.'

'So he's still around. Where?'

'Not in town. You won't find him, Ben, unless you stay. If you do that . . .'

'I know,' Ben said. 'They'll gun me down. But why? What makes me important?'

'I don't know that either.'

He looked at her narrowly. 'There's an outlaw band riding the basin. What are they after? Who's their leader?'

'I don't know of any. If there is one it might be Brazos and he's dangerous, Ben—even if he did hurt his hand. I've heard a rumor that he's better with his left hand than his right. He told one of the girls, two days ago, that you wouldn't live another day. He said you—then Lorimer.'

'Lorimer? Why Lorimer?'

'I'm not sure, Ben. Maybe he was just talking.'

A sudden thought ran through Ben's mind. Brazos had tried to get Ben with the ambush, then he said he'd get Lorimer next. When was Lorimer's turn. Tonight? The extra men Lorimer had brought in were gone. He might have a few men left, but Ben couldn't even be sure of that.

He said, 'Thanks, Laura.'

'If that means you're leaving, I'm glad,' Laura said. 'If you're pulling out of the basin you might even make it.'

He found José near the front door, and sent him after Milo. While Ben waited, he realized that the pattern for which he was hunting was beginning to show itself. Ackerman had told him that the strangers who had moved into the basin kept their horses in his livery, and they rode out at night. Five had pulled out tonight, shortly after dark. Five wasn't much of a crowd, but Milo had said that the men who had ambushed them had counted on surprise rather than numbers.

Milo showed up, grumbling. 'You sure hurried things up. I had hardly any time with Irma.'

'You can see her again.'

'Sure, but she felt like talking. She knew Taft, the man you shot in the saloon. She knew Wells, who died at Matthews' house tonight.

159

He was one of Brazos' crowd. That was what she called them.'

'And that ties in George Matthews,' Ben said, nodding. 'We've got some riding to do—to Lorimer's.'

'To Lorimer's! Why?'

'Didn't you say you wanted to catch up with the men who ambushed us?'

'Damned right. Are they going to hit Lorimer's?'

'We might be too late.'

'Then we'll ride like hell,' Milo said, and he started in the direction of Ackerman's livery stable.

*　　　*　　　*

They rode up the basin, cutting across country, and while they were still quite a distance from Lorimer's they started hearing the sounds of rifle fire. There was a lot of it, but as they drew nearer the sounds faded, then stopped.

'We'll be too late,' Milo said, and he added some profanity. Then he said, 'Maybe they'll still be around.'

A red glow showed up on the horizon. It grew brighter, blossomed higher into the night sky. It thinned the deep shadows, tinted them in color.

'Bastards!' Milo shouted. 'They've set the place afire.'

Ben nodded, and kept riding. Here was

160

another fire, similar to what had happened to his place. They were now near enough to see the flames licking into the air. There were several fires—the ranch house, the barn, the bunkhouse, the sheds—everything was burning. Off to the side at the edge of the light were several mounted men. They seemed to be watching the fire—that was all.

Ben pointed. 'Look over there.'

'Just what I wanted,' Milo answered. 'Some of them waited. We'll take them.' He swung his horse in that direction.

But even as Ben and Milo headed in that direction the men turned away, started off. Not far away was a thin stand of timber, where they could be lost.

Ben reined up. He shouted, 'No, Milo. Back to the fire.'

'We can ride them down,' Milo yelled.

'Not on our horses,' Ben answered. 'We've been pushing them too hard. We'll go after the men later.'

He headed back toward the burning buildings. Milo hesitated, but then followed him.

They rode closer to the fire, then suddenly Ben rode faster. The front door of the main house had been closed, but it opened abruptly and a man staggered out. He blundered across the porch, reached the steps, started down them. When he was almost at the bottom he lost balance, sprawling into the yard. He tried to get up but couldn't make it.

Ben rode in as far as he thought he could, then he swung to the ground and went on by foot. Milo kept right behind him. It was like walking into an oven. It was blisteringly hot, but they reached Lorimer, picked him up, then hurried him away. He was bleeding from a shoulder wound. When they were safely away from the heat they lowered him to the ground.

Milo looked around. 'Don't see anyone else.'

'Jeff might have been alone,' Ben said.

He opened the man's shirt. It didn't look too serious, if the bleeding could be stopped.

'I'd better catch our horses,' Milo said.

'Do that,' Ben said. 'Then see if you can catch another horse. There ought to be a few around. One of the raiders opened the corral.'

'A horse for Lorimer?' Milo shook his head. 'He's in no shape to ride a horse.'

'He'll manage it,' Ben said. 'He's got to. What do you suppose this is all about? Lorimer's supposed to be dead. We've got to get him away from here.'

'All right. See what I can do,' Milo said.

Ben was thinking faster than ever. The pattern was clearer. Matthews wanted this land. He had already promised half of it to the two Texans. The rest he would sell to someone else. But to do that and to satisfy the Texans, Jeff Lorimer had to die. He was supposed to have died tonight in a raging fire.

There were other things to fit into the pattern. Jeff had no close relatives. He might not have any at all. If he died suddenly, and if Matthews said that Jeff had sold half his range, who could prove that he was wrong? He could write up the sale, could copy Jeff's signature from the bank files. In four more days the Texans were going to drive their cattle south, onto land they had just bought.

Ben knelt down at Jeff's side. He tore off part of his shirt, made a pack and pressed it against the wound in Jeff's shoulder. The man needed a doctor, and some quiet care. But the greatest danger Jeff faced lay in the fact that someone might discover he was still alive.

Ben worked quickly, finished a crude but workable bandage and got it in place. Milo had their two horses, but he hadn't found another. When the corral had been opened, the horses there had fled.

'Then we'll put Lorimer on my horse,' Ben decided. 'I'll ride behind him. That'll be better, anyhow.'

'Where we going?' Milo asked.

'To town.'

'To town? Are you crazy?'

'No, but we've got to make it before dawn, so we better get started.'

'Are we going to Ackerman's?'

'That's right—the barn. The next few days might be interesting.'

'You can bet on that,' Milo said.

163

Jeff Lorimer was still unconscious. They boosted him into the saddle, and started away. The fires were still burning. They might burn for another hour. Nothing would be left of the Lorimer buildings by morning, excepting mounds of gray ashes, and here and there charred timbers.

And in town . . .

Ben was grimly looking forward to that. They would find their answers in town.

XII

It was Rod Ackerman who went after Doc Paisley with the story of a wonderful horse he could buy. 'He's cheap—only fifteen dollars,' Ackerman said. 'But you gotta move now.'

The doctor took the fifteen dollars with him—and his bag. He was never without it.

'Come on around here,' Ackerman said, and he led the doctor in back of his stacked, baled hay.

Three men were there—Ben, standing guard; Milo, asleep; and Jeff Lorimer, unconscious.

Paisley gasped, then he looked at Ackerman. 'I—I don't understand.'

'Don't try,' Ackerman said. 'Just do what you can for Jeff.'

Paisley was reputed to be a good doctor. He knew his job. He got down on his knees now and got to work.

Jeff woke up while this was happening, and he asked weakly, 'How'd I get here?'

'Don't ask me,' Paisley answered. 'From what I heard in town, you got burned to death when your house burned down.'

'Damned near did,' Jeff said.

His eyes shifted, he saw Ben and his face set in hard, tight, uncompromising lines. After a moment he asked, 'Doc, am I going to make it?'

'You'll make it if you take it easy,' Paisley said.

'Good,' Jeff said. 'There are four men I want to run down.'

'There are more than four,' Ben said. 'And they're mine.'

'No. They're mine,' said Milo, who'd awoke when the doctor came in.

Jeff closed his eyes. He opened them in a moment, stared at Ben and asked, 'Did you bring me here?'

'Me and Milo.'

'Where did you find me?'

'You got out of the house yourself. We picked you up in the yard.'

The man was silent for a moment, then said, 'All right, I gotta thank you for that—but that's all. Give me a gun and I'll be all right.'

'I'll get you a gun,' Ben said. 'But I want you to lay there for three days, getting your strength back. The buzzards will be getting together. Maybe you can go with us, bust up their celebration.'

'More trouble for me,' Paisley said, and he looked at Ben. 'Don't wave your gun at me. I won't be talking about who's in the barn. Rod Ackerman might get hurt—and he's been promising me for months that he'd get me a good buggy horse. Maybe, someday, he'll remember it.'

'I'll get you one of the best,' Ben said.

'Huh,' the man grunted and looked down at Lorimer. 'You just lay there on your blankets and take it easy.'

* * *

The day passed. Andy Thorne came in to get his horse. He had ridden out last night on some errand, had seen the glow of the fire on the horizon and had hurried to the Lorimer ranch. He was the first to bring word that Lorimer had died in the destruction of his buildings.

A rider from the east basin told Ackerman that Ben had fled the country. Two others said the same. Apparently someone at Laura's had started the rumor. Laura Digby, herself, might have been responsible.

Doc Paisley dropped by after dark. He seemed pleased with Jeff's condition. He came by the next morning, changed the bandage and said that Jeff could start eating solid food, then he scowled and said, 'What are you doing about food?'

'We'll work things out,' Ackerman said.

'I'll talk to my wife,' Paisley said. 'Have her cook up a stew. I'll drive my buggy in late this afternoon, and deliver it. And don't worry. My wife won't talk.'

'That'll help a lot, Doc.'

'Just hope I'm not doing wrong,' Paisley said.

They had more news by noon. Rumor had it that Jeff Lorimer had signed a deed, turning over the north half of his range to Chico Kelly and Eddie Bryan. The sale had been arranged two days ago and was to have become effective in five days. George Matthews, who had arranged the sale just before Lorimer's unfortunate death, had announced that the terms of agreement would be fulfilled. The money the Texans had paid for the land would be given to Lorimer's heirs.

'I don't have any heirs,' Jeff said gruffly. 'And I never sold an acre, to anyone. This whole thing is a lie. I want to see Matthews.'

'We'll see him—in two days,' Ben said.

'I want to see him now.'

'He's only part of the crowd, Jeff.'

'How you gonna get them together?'

'Maybe I won't. We'll have to see what happens. We've got two more days.'

'I don't want to wait two days.'

Ben said, 'I want you to think about what's going to happen to the cattle north of your place.'

'Hell with them.'

'That doesn't graze them.'

'I'm not gonna graze them. They'll stay off my land.'

Ben shook his head. 'You don't use half your range.'

'Someday I will.'

'But not now. You could lease a quarter of

168

your range. It wouldn't hurt it a bit and you could pick up a little extra money.'

'I don't need money that bad.'

'Think about it, anyhow,' Ben said. 'Someone's got to graze those extra cattle.'

Another day passed, and late in the afternoon Ackerman came in with the news Ben had been waiting to hear. The Texans were riding in the next morning. They would meet with Matthews, make a final payment and would receive a deed to cover the new range they were buying. By noon the extra cattle would be moving south.

'We're too late,' Lorimer said angrily.

Ben shook his head. 'No. Cattle can always be moved. What is important is the certification of a man's property rights. You own the land that's being sold. You can claim it as yours. We'll attend that meeting tomorrow morning—if we can reach it.'

'We'll reach it,' Lorimer said.

He was still a sick man. His wound was draining. He could stand up, but wasn't steady on his feet. He had moments of dizziness. He could probably go through a mild experience with no trouble—but the meeting in the morning might turn out to be rough. Ben had the feeling the outlaws might be somewhere around, wanting to be paid. Andy Thorne probably would be there as acting sheriff. Tomorrow morning might not be easy on anyone.

'We'll use the wagon tomorrow morning,' he said. 'I'll drive it. Jeff and Milo can lie in the bed of the wagon under blankets. Once we reach the bank we'll move right in.'

'No, I'll drive the wagon,' Milo said.

'I'll drive it,' Ackerman said. 'After all, it's my wagon—and my team. And I can still use a gun if it's needed. Reckon I'll go to the meeting.'

'You don't have to, Rod.'

'Then don't rule me out.'

Lorimer sat up. He closed his eyes for a moment, then said, 'Just get me to the bank. I can tell Matthews where to get off. I don't need any of you.'

'Stubborn cuss, ain't he?' Milo said.

'Mean too,' Ackerman said. 'Sometimes he even hates himself.'

Lorimer shook his head grimly. 'Just wait until I get on my feet.'

'You might never make it,' Ben said. 'And we're not helping you tomorrow. We got into this fight, ourselves, and we're trying to finish it. If you got pulled in yourself, that's your fault. Why don't we all shut up till morning?'

Lorimer settled down on his blanket. If he didn't fall asleep, he seemed to. Ackerman got busy in another part of the barn. Milo dug out a deck of cards and started playing solitaire. Ben sat down in the corner and it occurred to him, wryly, that he had made no plans to leave the bank or to escape. That meant he was resting everything on what happened during the meeting. It was like putting up all he had on one card—an all or nothing bet.

He scowled and shook his head. Everything couldn't work out that simply. They still had to decide where to graze the extra cattle. After you smashed something down, then you had to rebuild. A battle didn't end things—it was used to point a direction.

*   *   *

The morning was clear, crisp and quiet. Ackerman came down early, started a fire in the corner of the saddling yard and made some coffee in a huge coffeepot. Then he started cooking eggs and bacon.

Doc Paisley came in to see Lorimer. The day before, in addition to looking at Lorimer, the doctor had taken a look at the wounds in Ben's scalp and arm, and concluded Ben was doing very well. This morning he looked only at Lorimer.

'Three more days and you can start moving around,' he said, nodding. 'But don't hurry it. I still want you to stay on your back.'

'I'll think about it,' Lorimer said.

'But don't think about moving,' Paisley said, and he turned away.

As he was leaving Tish Wellington rode in, leading another horse. She dismounted, handed her reins to Ackerman and said, 'This

171

other horse belongs to Kate. We'll be riding some time this afternoon.'

'Anytime,' Ackerman said. 'I'll be around.'

She nodded, then asked, 'Where's Ben?'

'Ben?'

'Yes. If anyone around here knows where he is . . .'

Ben, who had been watching from inside the door, called out, 'That's all right, Rod. Bring her in.'

Ackerman didn't have the chance to do that. The girl hurried past him, saw Ben just inside the door, and no one else, and moved right into his arms.

He approved that very much. He held her close, whispering her name. He was thinking it would be a wonderful thing to be greeted like this every time he came home, and if things worked out this morning maybe he could arrange it.

'Well, I'll be damned,' Ackerman said, peering into the barn.

'You can look the other way,' Ben said. 'This is approved.'

He held her for a time but then he pushed her away and said, 'I thought you were going back to the mesa.'

'I did mean to,' Tish answered, 'but I was worried about Kate. I didn't think you'd be going back to the house so I did—just to see if she was there. And she was, but she was sick, shocked, terrified. I think for a while she was

172

out of her mind. I had to stay with her, Ben. I couldn't leave her. I even had to make her eat.'

'How is she now?'

'Better. But different than she used to be. She's older—much older. I mean she seems to be older. She still has traces of anger, but it doesn't hold up. She's never said anything about Dave or Carl or Hank, but when we heard that Lorimer was dead she said, "I could have stopped that." And right away she wanted to come to town. We got up quite early. I think she wants to see Mr. Matthews. And she wants you. She said you were supposed to be working for her.'

'Where's Kate now?'

'On the hotel porch, close to the bank.'

'And how did you know what happened to Lorimer?'

'Andy Thorne rode by. I think he was really looking for you. He said you hadn't been seen for days. How do you think that made me feel?'

He grinned at her. 'You're not supposed to worry about me.'

'Then I won't. How do you like that?'

'Will you do one thing for me?'

'What?'

'Let Kate go to the bank alone. I have a reason for that, Tish.'

'Then I'll try to stay away. When am I going to see you?'

'Maybe tonight.'

173

'Tonight.' Her eyes brightened.

'Yes, I think tonight,' Ben said. And he took her in his arms.

*　　*　　*

Tish didn't stay long. She hurried back to Kate and after she left Ben wondered why Kate wanted to see Matthews, and why she had said she could have saved Lorimer. Maybe she knew what Matthews had been planning; she might even have been a part of the scheme, but Ben didn't want to think so.

He checked the time. It was almost eight-thirty. Every business set its own hours. Matthews usually opened his bank by nine o'clock. It was time to get the wagon ready.

Ackerman, who had walked to the plaza and back, was frowning as he hitched up his wagon. 'There's too many strangers in town,' he told Ben. 'There's four of them in the plaza, across from the bank. And Brazos is there, his right hand still bandaged and his holster on the left side.'

'Are the Texans here?' Ben asked.

'Not yet, but they'll be pulling in early. You can count on that.'

'How about Andy Thorne?'

'Didn't see him, but that don't mean anything.'

Ben took another look at his watch and nodded. 'I'll get the others. It's time to get started up the street.'

Lorimer had insisted on two guns. He had one in his holster, one in his coat pocket. Milo had two guns, as did Ben. Ackerman had one that anyone could see. He wasn't supposed to be involved, anyhow.

'This is gonna be my meeting,' Lorimer said gruffly, as he moved toward the wagon.

'We'll all take part in it,' Ben said. 'But don't worry about that. When you walk in, no one's gonna see anything else.'

'Did you say Kate was gonna be there? Why?'

'I don't know, Jeff. Do you?'

'Hell with her,' Lorimer said. 'Let's go.'

They got in the bed of the wagon under some blankets. Ackerman was doing the driving to the plaza and around to the bank. He would move the wagon as near to the bank's door as possible. When he got there he would let them know, and would tell them who was standing around.

Ben spent an uncomfortable time while the wagon rolled up the street to the plaza. It took longer than he thought it would. He had been on edge when the trip started. By the time Ackerman stopped the wagon he was ready for anything.

Rod called out, 'Whoa! Whoa!' And when the wagon came to a stop, Rod's voice was low, steady. 'Nobody cluttering the door. The Texans are here, their horses are at the tie-rail just ahead. Don't see Brazos or Andy Thorne, but there's six or seven men watching me— men I don't know.'

'Then here we go,' Ben said. 'Milo, you get out first, help Jeff over the wheel. Me and Ackerman will follow you.'

He threw off the blanket that had been covering him, stood up and drew his gun, but he didn't lift it. He wouldn't use his gun unless it was necessary.

Milo was quickly out from the blankets. He never stood up; he seemed to roll over the side of the wagon and over the wheel. He landed on his feet, stood waiting to help Lorimer, and Lorimer moved pretty fast.

Ben was aware of what they were doing, but he was more interested in the men who were watching. There was a group on the boardwalk just beyond the bank. There was another group on the other side of the door. Three in the first group, five in the other. Ben recognized two of the three, Pancho Cos and Lou Jerrod. They were two of the three men he had jailed, men who had been released by Brazos. Momentarily these men were startled as they watched the men emerge from the wagon. No one grabbed for a gun.

Lorimer reached the ground. He started to the bank, Milo walking with him, ready to help him. In another moment they'd reach the door.

'Time for us to move, Rod,' Ben said. 'What

do you say we hurry?'

'Like this!' Ackerman said, and he was out of the seat and down on the ground fast.

Ben followed him. One of the men up the street seemed to suddenly wake up to the fact that things were going wrong. He clawed up his gun, snapped a shot at Ben. The bullet was high. Ben was down on the ground by this time, racing for the door. He heard two more shots as he reached the door, just behind Ackerman. There was no delay at that point. The door to the bank was open. He moved inside, closed it.

There were two bank employees back of the grilled cages. Andy Thorne was there, back of the railing and back of Matthews' desk. Ben gave him a passing glance and then his eyes came to rest on Matthews and the two Texans. They were standing, dumbly their eyes fixed on Lorimer, who had reached the railing and was leaning there.

For a moment no one spoke.

It was Ackerman who broke the silence. He had moved on to the railing near Ben. He spoke directly to Andy. 'Touch your gun, and I'll kill you.'

Andy had moved his hand toward his gun, but when Ackerman spoke he drew his hand back.

'Thanks, Rod,' Ben said, and he raised his voice. 'Matthews, I think you know Lorimer. He owns some property you're selling. Isn't that why the two Texans are here?'

'Sure, that's why I'm here,' Chico Kelly said. 'I thought Lorimer was dead, but I'm sure glad I was wrong.'

'That so?' Lorimer switched his attention from Matthews to Kelly. 'I'm not selling you a damned acre.'

Kelly scowled. 'How about that, Matthews? You told me Lorimer had changed his mind.'

Matthews gulped. He didn't say a word.

'Damn it, Matthews, you made a bargain with me,' Kelly said. 'You promised me land— as much as we needed. I even put up half the money.'

Matthews tried again. 'I—I—'

'Damn it, say something,' Kelly shouted. 'I've got twenty-five hundred cattle that need graze. Where am I gonna send them?'

'Let me say something.' Ben moved forward. 'If Matthews promised you land, then he promised something he didn't have. Of course, if Jeff Lorimer had been killed in that fire, I guess he could have sold it. Could be that was the reason for the fire.'

'No! No! I didn't have anything to do with that fire,' Matthews said shrilly. He could finally talk. He had to. 'I—I thought maybe Kate would sell some of her land. I thought—'

'You thought!' Kelly was still shouting. 'You thought—but where am I gonna put my cattle? That's what I want to know.'

The street door started opening. Milo raced

178

that way but he wasn't quick enough. He grabbed his gun, but then lowered it as Kate stepped inside—Iron Kate, and some of the iron was still there.

She marched forward, but stopped when she saw Lorimer, frowned, and said, 'Huh! So they didn't get you. What did you do—sell out?'

Lorimer slashed his arm through the air. 'Sell out? Me? Never! You ought to know me better'n that.'

She pointed to Matthews. 'You came to me for land. I said no and you said if I could hold a line at the river, you'd put enough pressure on Lorimer to make him sell. I know what you did. You hired them outlaws, but why did you turn them on me? I want to know.'

The banker moistened his lips. 'I don't know what you're talking about. Outlaws? I've got nothing to do with any outlaws.'

'How about Brazos Fowler?'

'He's no outlaw. He even served here as sheriff. If he was here he could tell you how I feel about outlaws.'

'All right, call him in,' Ben said. 'He's just outside.'

'I'll do that,' Matthews said.

He got up, moved through the gate in the counter and headed for the door.

'I wouldn't go outside,' Milo said, who was near the door. 'There's some rough-looking characters outside. Just open the door and call Brazos—and I'll bet he doesn't answer.'

179

'He's a fine man,' Matthews said.

He reached the door, opened it, then did a strange thing—he started running, shouting, 'Brazos! Brazos!' He turned to the right and almost at once disappeared from sight.

Milo hurried to close the door. There was a shot down the street, just one, but Ben was thinking that this was just the beginning.

He turned toward the two Texans. 'The land you expected to buy isn't here. Matthews lied to you.'

Chico shook his head angrily. 'I don't care about that. We're gonna get graze for our cattle.'

'No land to buy,' Ben said. 'But maybe you can lease some land—from Lorimer and Kate.'

'Never!' Kate snapped.

'That's what I say.' Lorimer nodded.

'We came to buy,' Chico said sharply.

'But you can't,' Ben said. 'And Lorimer and Kate, both, have land they're not using. They might as well lease it. What's the matter with you people—all of you? Do you want to keep this war running—want more people to get killed? Sit down and start talking.'

'We got nothing to say.' Kate glared at him. 'Ain't you working for me?'

'Yep, but this is the way I work,' Ben said. 'How about leasing the north third of your range?'

*   *   *

180

It took a lot of talk, but in a few hours they worked out the framework of a lease agreement. It would be for only a year. There might be trouble after it was over, or earlier, but they were talking and if they kept on talking there was less chance of conflict.

Milo talked to Ben near the door. 'Those men are still outside. We're gonna have to shoot our way out.'

'Then we will, the Texans with us,' Ben said, and he looked around. 'Where's Andy Thorne?'

'I saw him near the back door.' Milo pointed. 'He must have slipped outside.'

Chico joined them. 'We're gonna get two leases, one from Lorimer, one from Kate. It isn't what I wanted but I guess it'll do. I reckon we've got to thank you for it.'

'Then live within it,' Ben said. 'And don't try to take over the basin. You could have known Matthews was trying to force someone to sell. I think you did.'

'But I didn't back him up in hiring outlaws,' Chico snapped. 'And I don't go for murder.'

'Then do you want to walk into the street with us?'

'Why not?'

'Might be trouble out there—Brazos and some of his men are waiting.'

'I'll call Eddie Bryan. We'll even walk ahead of you when we go out. How's that?'

'Just keep up with me,' Ben said.

*   *   *

They moved outside a little while later, Ben and Chico leading the way, Milo and Eddie Bryan just behind them, and trailing them, moving together for a change, Jeff Lorimer and Iron Kate. Ackerman was last.

There was a brief gunfight in the street. Brazos and four of his men were to one side of the bank; there were three on the other side. Those men left right after the first shots—that is, two of them left. One man didn't. He dropped and stayed there.

Brazos stayed until he was smashed to the ground. The four men with him didn't. Three were dropped as they fled down the street. The fourth escaped, but he was thought to be wounded.

*   *   *

Tish was waiting for Ben, right on the fringe of the trouble, and when she could she joined him.

She was shaky. 'Is it all over?'

'I think so. I'm not sure about Matthews—'

'He's dead,' Tish answered. 'I think it was Brazos who shot him. Someone said Brazos shouted, "Where's my money?" Then he grabbed his gun. Another thing. I saw Andy

Thorne. He's gone. He said I was to tell you he's sort of sorry he got mixed up in what happened. Does that make sense?'

'Yes, I guess it does,' Ben said.

She tugged at his arm. 'Let's go.'

'Where?'

'Anywhere you'll be safe.'

'Where's my money?'

'At Kate's—hidden.'

'Then we'll go there. We can use one of the cabins. Don't you want to get married?'

'Can we do it right away?'

He looked at her curiously. 'What kind of a woman are you?'

'The kind of woman who wants you to be safe,' Tish answered. Then she smiled. 'There are other things about me, too. I don't think you're going to be disappointed.'

He wouldn't be. He knew that. He had some work to do for Kate, then a ranch to rebuild. Tish would be with him and Milo would be there to help.

It would be a good life.

We hope you have enjoyed this Large Print book. Other Chivers Press or Thorndike Press Large Print books are available at your library or directly from the publishers.

For more information about current and forthcoming titles, please call or write, without obligation, to:

Chivers Large Print
published by BBC Audiobooks Ltd
St James House, The Square
Lower Bristol Road
Bath BA2 3BH
UK
email: bbcaudiobooks@bbc.co.uk
www.bbcaudiobooks.co.uk

OR

Thorndike Press
295 Kennedy Memorial Drive
Waterville
Maine 04901
USA
www.gale.com/thorndike
www.gale.com/wheeler

All our Large Print titles are designed for easy reading, and all our books are made to last.